"I thought I'd lost you."

Dominic breathed in a whisper of yearning that found a deep echo inside Carrie. "Lost you forever." Then in a burst of relief, "But it's not so. Thank God it's not so."

His arms tightened around her. His lips trailed down to her ear. "You can't deny me now, Carrie," he pleaded softly. "Say you love me."

The words were there, embedded in her heart. Carrie wanted to say them. She had promised herself she would speak only the truth to Dominic. Had to speak the truth. And her body had already betrayed that truth, anyway. Yet the memory of what had happened last time came back to haunt her. It was all too one-sided. Where was his commitment to her? He asked too much. And he would leave her to go back to his wife, his marriage.

EMMA DARCY nearly became an actress until her fiancé declared he preferred to attend the theater *with* her. She became a wife and mother. Later, she took up oil painting—unsuccessfully, she remarks. Then she tried architecture, designing the family home in New South Wales. Next came romance writing—"the hardest and most challenging of all the activities," she confesses.

Books by Emma Darcy

HARLEQUIN PRESENTS
1288—THE ULTIMATE CHOICE
1335—TOO STRONG TO DENY
1351—ONE-WOMAN CRUSADE
1385—THE COLOUR OF DESIRE
1401—RIDE THE STORM
1433—BREAKING POINT

HARLEQUIN ROMANCE
2900—BLIND DATE
2941—WHIRLPOOL OF PASSION
3085—PATTERN OF DECEIT

EMMA DARCY

high risk

Harlequin Books

TORONTO • NEW YORK • LONDON
AMSTERDAM • PARIS • SYDNEY • HAMBURG
STOCKHOLM • ATHENS • TOKYO • MILAN
MADRID • WARSAW • BUDAPEST • AUCKLAND

Harlequin Presents first edition April 1992
ISBN 0-373-11447-8

HIGH RISK

CHAPTER ONE

SHE HAD TO GO TO HIM.

The idea had been nagging at Carrie's mind for days, and she had kept pushing it away. The last thing she wanted to do was go to Dominic Savage for help. But she had already tried everything else. There was no other option left. Or none that Carrie could see.

Dominic would be able to get Danny out of the clutches of those officious welfare people. All it would probably take was a telephone call to the right person. From him. The rules and regulations, which were so cast-iron for unimportant people like herself, were always bent to accommodate those with power and wealth and influence. Carrie had seen that happen too many times to have any doubt about it.

Bitter times forced bitter decisions, she reflected. The wealth and power in Dominic's world had once evoked awe in her, until she learnt that they also excluded her from ever being a permanent fixture in his life. Since it had cost her dear in the past, Carrie felt she had a right to use it now. For Danny's sake, more than her own. And only just this once.

She would be running a risk—a high risk—inviting even this slight involvement with Dominic Savage. Any association with him had to be strictly contained to today's meeting. Carrie didn't want old wounds re-opened. All she wanted was a quick efficient solution to her problem. With no follow-up. She had quite enough to cope with without any more disastrous repercussions from her move back to Australia.

She wished she had stayed in Fiji where at least she had friends. It was so lonely in Sydney with her mother gone and Danny taken away and no one she knew well enough to even pass the time of day with. Yet there was no way in the world she could have foreseen what had happened since her return. However, *if only* thoughts were a total waste of time, Carrie told herself sternly.

The question to be faced was, considering the nature of their brief relationship, would Dominic Savage help her?

Because she remembered him, it didn't follow that he remembered her. Eight years was a long time, and for him it had only been a holiday fling. After she had found out what was really happening, she had ended it there and then. Even left the country to get farther away from him.

Had he married the other girl?

She didn't even know anything as basic as that about him.

A bleak shadow passed over Carrie's soul. She shook it off. What Dominic Savage had done with his personal life was not her problem. Her problem was getting her child back. There was no point in worrying whether Dominic would remember her or not. If she had to, she would tell him who she was and make him remember. He was the only person she knew that she could turn to, and when she considered what was happening to her, surely to heaven it wasn't much to ask of him.

She would have to go to his office, Carrie decided. Calling him would be useless. It was all too easy to refuse a telephone call when the name given might not mean anything to him any more. Even in person, he might not recognise her, but she would not be turned away without seeing him first.

She pushed herself up from the bed, moving slowly so as not to bring on the awful dizziness quick action invariably triggered. This lingering weakness was a source of intense frustration.

She had never had a serious illness in her whole life, never had a day off work through sickness—until now. To be struck down by viral pneumonia just when she needed everything to go right was the cruellest trick Fate could have played on her. And this convalescence period was dragging on far too long. She had to get well again, and quickly. So the sooner she forced herself to move, the better off everyone would be.

She searched through her wardrobe for the most suitable thing to wear. Pride insisted that she look her best for the meeting with Dominic. In her present state it was clearly impossible to look her *absolute* best, but she had to do her utmost to look her *relative* best.

She had lost so much weight that all her clothes hung loosely on her. Carrie finally chose a green and white dotted cotton shirtwaist. It had a belt she could pull in and long sleeves to cover the thinness of her arms. Having to bend over to put on panty hose made her head whirl, but she managed to get them on eventually. The white low-heeled sandals were not exactly dressy, but she didn't feel safe in high heels, not with the balance problem she had at the moment.

She grimaced at the reflection that looked back at her from the bathroom mirror. Her face looked older than its twenty-seven years, tired and drained of any healthy youthful bloom. Her dark blond hair was no longer lightly streaked from the sun. It hung lifelessly to her shoulders and badly needed a good cut. She brushed it hard but couldn't get any shine into it. It felt like straw.

Carrie had never been in the habit of wearing much make-up. Never needed it. She only had a couple of lipsticks, so there was nothing she could do about adding some artificial lustre to her green eyes, or even putting some healthier-looking colour onto her pallid skin. She tried rubbing a smear of lipstick over her cheekbones, but it gave her a garish appearance, which looked even worse. She cleaned it off.

It was one o'clock when she left the dingy little apartment in Ashfield. She was glad to be out in the sunshine for a while. It had appalled her that such a dark, depressing place was all she could afford in the high-rental climate.

Of course, she hadn't anticipated remaining there beyond the three-month probation period of the job she had secured before coming back to Sydney. Assistant chef at a well-reputed restaurant paid well enough for her to find better accommodation, but Carrie's natural caution insisted that she be frugal until she was sure of permanent status on the staff. Which was just as well, since she had only been working for a week before going off sick. She couldn't blame the management for not holding the position for her, but if she didn't get well enough to hold a job soon, she would have to move to cheaper and worse accommodation.

It was bitterly ironic that when she had been in Fiji, she had been homesick for Australia. Now she yearned for what she had left behind. Fiji was a fine place. The sun was almost always shining. The cost of living was low. The Fijians were the friendliest people in the world. But living there for six years had not prepared her for the high cost of housing in Sydney, forced to astronomical heights by the huge Japanese investments in property. Still, Carrie refused to give in to pessimism. Today was the day. She was going to get Danny back, no matter what it cost her to do it.

It took her an hour to reach the huge APIC building in Bridge Street. One bus went straight past her. The next was so crowded she had to stand in the aisle for part of the way. Then she alighted at the wrong stop and had to walk three blocks. It was slow going with all the halts she had to make as she fought off waves of dizziness. When she finally reached her destination, Carrie was exhausted.

In times gone past the APIC building had dominated the Circular Quay area. Now it was just one of the many skyscrapers that comprised the inner-city business district. Nevertheless, it was still imposing. There was certainly nothing derelict about the polished marble exterior, nor the rich gleaming Jarrah woodwork and marble in the foyer.

She read the directory on the wall beside the bank of elevators, then rode up to the first floor, which was designated Reception and Inquiries. She stepped out into a spacious area that spelled prosperity in capital letters, took a deep breath to steady herself, then approached the long inquiry desk behind which several smartly dressed young women were working.

"How can I help you?" one of them asked, greeting Carrie with a polite smile.

"I'm here to see Mr. Savage," Carrie said, adopting a brisk, confident manner. "Could you please direct me to his office?"

"Take the elevator to the twenty-seventh floor. The receptionist there will direct you to the managing director's suite," the woman supplied helpfully.

"I meant Mr. Dominic Savage, not his father."

The woman gave her an odd questioning look. "Mr. Dominic Savage is now the managing director. He took over two years ago when Mr. James Savage died," she added pointedly.

Carrie stared blankly at her, slowly absorbing this new item of knowledge. She had thought of Dominic Savage frequently enough in the intervening years, but never of specific events happening to him. At least, nothing like the death of his father.

Of course Dominic's life had moved on, just as hers had. Eight years was a long time. She had lost her mother. He had lost his father. And now he was in an even more exalted position than she had imagined him to be. Nevertheless, that didn't change anything. In fact, the more important the position he held, the more influence he could wield. If he would. He had the power now, as well as the name.

"Thank you," she murmured, and headed to the elevators, conscious of the woman's eyes boring into her back. Carrie wondered if a call would precede her to the twenty-seventh floor, giving a warning that someone very strange was on the way up.

When she arrived, however, that anxiety was quickly erased. The receptionist apparently had no compunction whatsoever about directing her along a wide corridor towards the managing director's suite. "You'll find Mrs. Coombe's office down there," she said, passing Carrie up the line of authority with the words, "Mrs. Coombe handles all Mr. Savage's appointments."

Carrie thanked her and moved down the corridor. This led to a large open waiting room, which was presided over by a middle-aged woman at a massive semicircular desk.

Mrs. Coombe was not a welcoming figure. She looked every inch the guardian of the citadel of power. Her iron-grey hair was cut short in a trim mannish style. Horn-rimmed spectacles added emphasis to steely grey eyes. Her stout body was encased in a professional black suit, and the cameo brooch that was pinned to her pristine white blouse was the only touch of femininity she apparently allowed. Her stern face did not crack the slightest smile. Carrie was subjected to sharp scrutiny as she approached the woman. She had the feeling that she was judged and found wanting. The woman's face assumed a superior condescending expression, which boded ill for Carrie's purpose.

"Good afternoon," Mrs. Coombe said crisply. Eyebrows rose fractionally as she added, "How can I help you?"

"I wish to see Mr. Dominic Savage," Carrie stated flatly. She was feeling ill again. It was all the movement, she supposed. Soon she would have to sit down and rest.

"You want to make an appointment?"

Carrie concentrated fiercely, willing her body to behave as it should. "No. I want to see him this afternoon," she said firmly. "As soon as possible, really."

"I'm afraid that's impossible, Miss...?"

"Miller. Caroline Miller."

"Miss Miller." The steel-grey eyes had swept over Carrie's fingers. The voice continued with a huff of exasperation. "Mr. Savage is a very busy man. His afternoon is already filled with appointments. If you'll state your business and give me a contact number, I'll confer with Mr. Savage when he's available and let you know when an appointment would be convenient."

Another evasive runaround. Just like at the welfare department. Carrie wondered why no one seemed to realise when something was very important. It goaded her into digging her toes in. She was not going to be stopped by red tape here. Dominic might turn her away, but she wouldn't be turned away by this woman or anyone else.

"I've come on a personal matter, Mrs. Coombe. An urgent personal matter," Carrie said emphatically. "Mr. Savage and I are old acquaintances. I appreciate the fact he is a busy man, but I'm prepared to wait until he can see me. I'll wait all afternoon, if necessary."

The grey eyes glittered with suspicion. "I'm acquainted with all Mr. Savage's friends, Miss Miller. Your name is *not* on my list."

No doubt she didn't measure up as an acquaintance, let alone a friend, Carrie thought with grim irony. It was all too obvious that she didn't have the wealth or the style or the presence of someone from the right strata of society. That had been the problem eight years ago. She had run away from it then. But she was no longer a naive, inexperienced nineteen-year-old. She was not going to run away from it now. This woman's opinion did not matter to her. Not one whit. Only Danny mattered.

Her head swam. She could feel her forehead going clammy and perspiration breaking out over her body. She had to concentrate very hard to produce a rebuttal to Mrs. Coombe's argument. "I've been out of the country for many years," she explained. "Mr. Savage would have no reason to give you my name, Mrs. Coombe. But if you'd be kind enough to tell him I'm here, I'm sure he won't turn me away."

She was not at all sure of that, but if she didn't exude confidence, her case was lost. And what alternatives did that leave her? None that Carrie could think of. Perhaps tomorrow she would get another idea.

"Mr. Savage is in conference," the woman said officiously. "I expect he will be there for another hour, Miss Miller, and I have the strictest instructions not to interrupt a conference. Except in the direst of emergencies."

That was precisely the situation as Carrie saw it, but she was not in a position either to explain it or to be demanding. "Then I'll wait until you can speak to him," she stated as matter-of-factly as she could.

"As you wish." Mrs. Coombe gave a cold little nod of dismissal towards a group of armchairs, then ignored Carrie's presence, dropping her gaze to whatever paperwork she was doing.

Carrie was glad to sit down at last. The strain of getting here was fast catching up with her. She needed a rest before coming face to face with Dominic Savage. Time to regather her meagre resources of energy. An hour was nothing when so much hung in the balance.

For a long while Carrie mentally rehearsed what she would say to him if she got to see him. If he still remembered her and was kind enough to see her. She

exhausted all the possible opening gambits at her disposal, and eventually her surroundings impinged on
her consciousness. The pale blue-grey and white de-
cor was very modern. Understated class. The paint-
ings on the walls were watercolours—undoubtedly
originals—and subtly suggestive of many things without being truly representational of anything.

The telephone on Mrs. Coombe's desk rang from
time to time. Carrie tensed as the woman answered its
summons, not knowing if they were incoming calls or
in-house communications. She eavesdropped un-
ashamedly. The secretary didn't once mention Dominic's name, handling each call with an air of assurance
and competent efficiency.

There were two sets of double doors leading off the
office waiting room, one to the right of where Carrie
sat, the other to the left of Mrs. Coombe's desk. She
suspected that the doors closest to the secretary would
lead to Dominic's office. She watched them, waiting
for them to open and emit the members of the conference.

But it was the other set of doors that were eventually thrust open, the silence abruptly broken by an ac-
companying burst of male voices. A phalanx of men
spilled into the room, spreading out near the doorway like a guard of honour for the man who emerged
last.

Carrie's heart squeezed tight at first sight of him. If
anything, Dominic Savage was more handsome in
maturity than when she had met him. Then she had
thought him the most handsome boy she had ever
seen, so compellingly attractive that she could hardly
stop looking at him; eyes so blue, face just the right
mixture of perfect features and strong masculinity,

and the intriguing dimple at the base of his chin to break the rather uncompromising power of his square jawline.

Now he was very much the man. Although he could not be taller than she remembered him, he looked bigger and broader, the lean athletic physique of his youth obviously having filled out over the years, lending him a formidable aura of authority. Even his thick black hair had been tamed into a short, stylish cut, which added to the impressive executive air that a formal business suit gave him.

He paused to speak to one of the men. Carrie pushed herself out of the armchair, her pulse leaping erratically at her temerity—or perhaps it was at seeing him again in the flesh. Whatever, if she brought herself to his notice, forced a meeting so that her presence could not be ignored... It was a chance to bypass the dragon of a woman who guarded his lair.

He finished speaking. His listener nodded. A satisfied smile curved his mouth as he moved forward again.

The blue eyes gave Carrie a swift cursory glance.

There was not the slightest flicker of recognition.

She was dismissed from his notice almost in the same moment he saw her, and the shock of that dismissal rendered Carrie speechless. He passed on by, heading for the doors on the other side of Mrs. Coombe's desk.

Carrie gazed helplessly after him, too stunned by his failure to acknowledge her to make any move. Somehow, in her heart of hearts, she had wanted Dominic to know her instantly. Despite the brevity of their relationship, despite the change in her appearance, despite the years. It hurt that he didn't. It hurt so much that she even forgot why she had come.

Suddenly he checked in mid-stride. His back stiffened. He half turned, subjecting Carrie to a sharp, searching look. It lasted only a second or two, but it was enough for Carrie's frozen heart to leap alive again, enough to make every inch of her skin prickle with an electric awareness, enough to unlock thoughts and emotions that she had no right to have.

His head jerked forward again, and so did his legs. "Mrs. Coombe. In my office please," he rapped out as he passed his secretary. He didn't pause or wait for her. He went straight into his office, leaving the door open for Mrs. Coombe to follow.

As she stood up from the desk, the dragon shot a quelling frown at Carrie, clearly warning her to stay precisely where she was and not make any trouble. Mr. Dominic Savage had not acknowledged her as an old acquaintance. A second glance meant nothing, particularly as it had been followed by a second dismissal. As far as Mrs. Coombe was concerned, Miss Caroline Miller was here under false pretences, and she would certainly get her comeuppance later for having disturbed Mrs. Coombe's peaceful existence with her intrusive behaviour.

The wild rush of adrenaline that had been stirred by Dominic's second look at her drained quickly away, leaving Carrie shaking. The cold sweat broke out again on her forehead. She flopped into the seat rather than sat down. She might have fallen down, and again she cursed the debilitating weakness that swept over her.

She tried to push away the feelings Dominic had evoked. She couldn't still love him. Not after all these years. That was impossible. She had so carefully controlled all those awful wilful feelings. It was crazy to want what they had once had together. And what was obviously impossible for them to share. It had only ever been on her side, anyway. To him she had been available, willing, a bit of fun to be enjoyed until his friends arrived. That was how he had used her. Now she was only a vague memory, jogged for a moment, then dismissed as not worth pursuing.

So much for that episode in her life!

For a few intensely bleak moments Carrie wished she could die right here and now. Then she remembered Danny and slowly gathered her purpose for living. What she had shared with Dominic Savage was dead long ago. She had always known that. It was stupid and self-defeating to let such feelings influence her.

Even though he hadn't recognised her, she had expected that, hadn't she? It didn't mean she should give up on Danny. There had to be another way. She would think of it. Tomorrow. In the meantime it was useless to stay here. It was another good idea gone wrong. And it had always had the potential to make trouble that she would rather avoid. She had been weak minded to even consider such a high-risk venture. Better to avoid it now.

She pushed herself out of the chair. Despite the ringing in her ears she pushed her feet one after the other down the corridor to the bank of elevators in the reception area. She stabbed a down button, then pressed her forehead against the cold marble wall. It seemed to help. The cloud of dots that jagged across the front of her brain seemed to slow down. She would be better soon.

"Miss Miller."

Carrie jerked her head up. Mrs. Coombe was breathing hard, as if she had run down the corridor after her. But that couldn't be right. Carrie had to be mistaken. Mrs. Coombe carried herself like a sentinel, with irreproachable dignity. She would never run anywhere.

"Mr. Savage will see you now," she announced, as though bestowing a great and undeserved privilege.

For a second or two Carrie couldn't take it in. Then a great tremor ran through her. It wasn't relief. Now the moment was upon her, she was gripped by an overwhelming fear that she wouldn't be able to handle the interview in the manner she had planned. Before she had seen Dominic. If she said the wrong thing now . . . but she mustn't. Too much was at stake.

"Miss Miller?" The secretary was frowning at her.

Carrie steadied herself as best she could. "Thank you," she pushed out through dry lips. Her legs were weak and shaky but she willed them to move down the corridor again. For Danny, she recited fiercely with each fateful step she took. Mrs. Coombe led the way to Dominic's office, opened the door for her, then stood aside to usher Carrie into his presence.

It was a large office—spacious and luxurious, as befitted the chief executive officer of APIC—but Carrie didn't take in any details. She only had eyes for the man whose help she needed. He was standing at a large window, which undoubtedly gave a panoramic view of Sydney, since they were on the twenty-seventh floor. His back was turned to her. Carrie noticed one hand clenching and unclenching at his side.

The door was closed quietly and discreetly behind her. Dominic turned at the sound, slowly, as though he didn't want to face her but was forcing himself to.

They stared at each other across the room, across the distance of eight long years.

She could feel his tension as he studied her, knew he was contrasting the Carrie now with the Carrie he remembered and finding quite a lot gone wrong. The intense scrutiny gave him no pleasure. The grim expression on his face attested to that.

"It's been a long time," he said quietly, the blue eyes probing hers like twin lasers, intent on boring through to her soul.

"Yes," she agreed, her voice barely a whisper. "Thank you for seeing me, Dominic."

"I couldn't believe it was you out there, Carrie. Not until Mrs. Coombe confirmed it."

"I thought you hadn't recognised me."

"I didn't. Not at first," he said with a touch of dry irony. "It takes a bit of getting used to."

Carrie worked some moisture into her mouth. She couldn't let the memories crowding in on her divert her from her purpose. She had to get on with it. "I won't take up much of your time," she blurted out. "I'm sorry for barging in on you like this. When you're so busy."

"Take all the time you need, Carrie," he invited softly. "Tell me...what you need."

She flushed at his kindness. "A few minutes, perhaps a little more..."

He frowned, obviously not caring for her dismissal of his generosity. "Is that sufficient to catch up on eight years?" he asked, projecting a light tone that was not reflected in his eyes. "Eight years and two months, if my memory serves me correctly."

Why Dominic should want "to catch up" Carrie couldn't imagine. Probably it was only a polite remark. Dominic's manners had always been more than gracious. Class and style, she reminded herself. They were qualities that had once fooled her into believing more than she should have.

In any event, she didn't want to talk about her life. Not what had happened to her in all that time. She didn't want to know what had happened to him, either. In fact, the less she knew the better. All these years she had shut him out of her mind and heart, not always successfully, and she didn't want a prolonged meeting with him now. It was too disturbing, unsettling, and fraught with too many pitfalls. She had to achieve her purpose and get out of here as soon as possible.

"Dominic, this isn't a…a social reunion," she said with an edge of desperation, her green eyes begging his indulgence. "I've come because I need your help. I didn't know anyone else who could do what needs to be done. You're my only chance. Otherwise I would never have intruded into your life."

"Of course. What else?" he murmured. The blue eyes gathered a cynical self-mockery. "I never thought your visit was connected to doing something for me, Carrie."

The rush of blood that had scorched her cheeks receded with devastating swiftness. Carrie knew that what had to be said and what had to be done had to be said and done quickly. She was feeling less and less in control of herself with each second that passed. She managed one step towards him, lifted her hand imploringly.

"I'm so sorry to be a nuisance—"

"You aren't." The quick retort was clipped. "What can I do for you?" The manner of his words was not harsh, but he looked so remote and controlled. He moved towards his desk, seeming to retreat from her.

"It's my baby..."

Close enough to the truth, Carrie thought. Danny was her baby. Always would be. However, the effect of her words on Dominic Savage was both instantaneous and incomprehensible. A bleak frozen stillness washed over him, enveloped him, making him appear rigid and stern.

I've lost this encounter, Carrie thought wildly. He's not going to help me at all. Was he judging her harshly for having a baby?

The floor tilted crazily. The black dots came swarming back. Not now, she told them.

"What about your baby?" The words were shot at her on a flat trajectory, totally devoid of emotion.

Carrie harnessed all her willpower to deliver the final message, and she managed to get the words out. "I want you to find Danny for me. I *need* you to get him back for me."

Then she was falling towards the thick grey cloud of carpet, and it came up to meet her halfway. She felt no pain at the contact. It felt warm and soft and comfortable and secure, like being wrapped in cotton wool. Just where I want to be, Carrie thought.

It was the last conscious thought Carrie had for quite some time.

CHAPTER TWO

SOMETHING COLD AND HARD was moving over her chest. It felt terrible, and Carrie wished it would go away. She didn't have the strength to push it away. She willed it to stop. It seemed to work. The cold hard object was abruptly removed.

She wondered about opening her eyes but decided against it. The effort required was too great. It was much, much easier to leave everything the way it was. She felt exactly right here. Warm. Comfortable. Heavenly, really. The best she had felt for quite some time.

Then she became aware of one intrusion. There were voices murmuring in the background. Carrie strained her ears to catch what was being said.

"What's the problem with her, doctor?"

That was Dominic Savage's voice. It carried a note of anxiety. Memory rushed into Carrie's consciousness. He probably thought I was going to die on him, she wildly surmised. And a death in his office would hardly be good for business. No wonder he's anxious!

But if doctors were involved, Carrie had to stir herself fast. It was the last thing she needed. She had already had far too much to do with doctors. She had to get up, get out of here, leave Dominic Savage behind and think of some other method for attacking this problem. She tried to move, then reflected that another minute or two of resting wouldn't do any harm.

"Hard to be certain, really."

That had to be the doctor's voice. Low and disembodied, and like all the doctors she had ever met, disinclined to be certain of anything. They just made her feel angry and frustrated. Carrie listened to his *uncertain* diagnosis.

"There is fluid on the lungs. The heart may be overstrained . . . diaphoresis . . ."

So it was a stethoscope that had been moving over her chest and causing her distress! She had learnt to hate stethoscopes in hospital. They were so coldly intrusive and impersonal. And she could never tell what the doctors learnt from them. They always hummed and hahed as though they were pontificating over something important but they never said anything definite.

"Without more tests it's impossible to be sure—" the doctor's faraway voice intoned.

Not more tests, Carrie promised him, with a violence of feeling that set adrenaline running through her veins.

"But my provisional diagnosis is that the basic problem is malnutrition."

What rot, Carrie thought.

"You must be joking!" Dominic's voice was filled with anger and disbelief.

Carrie silently approved.

"Take one look at her!" the doctor said pointedly.

So I'm too thin, Carrie conceded reluctantly, but it's not my fault I can't find much appetite these days. All the same, I must try and eat more, she told herself.

There was a disquieting silence.

"That's my opinion until tests confirm it or disprove it," the doctor went on.

"What are you going to do about it?" Dominic asked with a tight thread of concern.

"I'll call an ambulance and get her admitted to Royal Prince Alfred Hospital. Then . . ."

Movement was instantly triggered by the well of protest that surged through Carrie. Her eyes flew open. She forced her limbs into action and managed to sit up. Her head swam. But she could see why she had been so comfortable. Not only was she on a soft leather sofa, but her head had been on a pillow and she had been swathed in blankets. Two male heads swivelled towards her.

"Not going!" Her voice was just a croak, but as far as she was concerned the tone was both incisive and decisive. From the very beginning, hospitals and doctors had created the problem she was having now. A repetition of that was too much to endure. In fact the more distance she put between them and her, the better chance she had of getting Danny back.

"Carrie, you heard what the doctor just said." There was a harsh edge of disbelief in Dominic's voice. "You have to do what he advises. In fact, you'll follow his advice to the letter!"

Carrie focussed on Dominic Savage. She had never seen him look like this before, dominating and imperious. She remembered him as always being easy and relaxed, full of camaraderie, gaiety and laughter. She shook her head. He didn't appreciate what was at stake here. But he did look very handsome and compelling with that authoritative look on his face.

"Not going," she repeated dully. She didn't really like going against his wishes. She just had to.

"Oh, yes you are!" His square jaw looked very determined. Even the dimple seemed to flatten out.

But Carrie was even more determined. She knew better. "Over my dead body!" she told him.

He looked even more grim at that. "It will be if you don't do as you're told."

Carrie decided he wasn't going to understand anything. "Sorry," she said, with a terribly leaden feeling in her heart. Somehow she dredged up the strength to stand up without falling over again. "Going home," she stated decisively.

Dominic seemed to lunge at her. Then his hands and arms were wrapped around her shoulders, steadying her, as if to protect her from falling again. Which could happen, she admitted to herself. She did feel weak and shaky.

"No ambulance," he conceded. "I'll take you to hospital myself."

"No. Going home," Carrie insisted. "Sorry for nuisance. Goodbye, Dominic."

For a moment she let herself lean against the warm breadth of his chest. It felt so good. She was just regaining her strength and balance. That was all. He had changed his after-shave lotion from what he used to use. She liked it, though. It was very...manly. She wondered if his hair still felt soft and springy. Like the curls on his chest. She could feel the hard muscular power of his thighs. Somehow that made her own even more quivery. Very weak.

"Carrie, you don't have any choice."

His voice had a raw, gravelly sound to it. Exasperation, she thought. She was being a lot of trouble to him. She had to make a stand and get it over with. She couldn't really fool herself that the weakness coursing through her was entirely due to her sickness. Dominic had always had a sort of melting effect on her.

But that had to stop. She was indulging herself when she should be thinking of Danny. Only Danny. And that meant no more doctors saying she was too sick to have her child back. And definitely no hospital. She forced some stiffening into her spine and lifted her head, meeting Dominic's eyes with defiant and unshakeable purpose.

"If you so much as try to force me..." She concentrated her mind as best she could. "I'll charge you with kidnapping, invasion of privacy, abduction and—" she searched desperately for some other threat "—deduction."

That last word wasn't quite right but somehow it fitted together into the general pattern. Perhaps she was getting light-headed. It was so important to get the right words.

The blue eyes seemed to sharpen in intensity. "Please, Carrie! For my sake!"

"Sorry!" She was definitely repeating herself. "Not for your sake, Dominic," she added for good measure.

"God damn it!" That raw, gravelly tone *was* exasperation. "You're being stupidly wilful! And impossible!"

"Yes," she agreed, not wanting to annoy him any further. "That's exactly right."

He kept one arm clamped around her shoulders as he swung to face the doctor. "Isn't there something we can do?" He seemed to be imploring for some authority from the medical profession.

Carrie wasn't going to take that. Not after her recent experiences!

"If the young lady is adamant...it is her right to refuse treatment. She cannot be forced," came the considered reply.

And about time someone recognised my rights, Carrie thought belligerently. If only she could get the welfare people to do the same thing, there wouldn't be a problem.

Dominic's chest heaved and fell. "Thank you for your time and trouble, Dr. Burridge," he said on a strained note of resignation. "I'll let you know when something can be done."

The doctor gave a rueful grimace. "I wish you luck."

Carrie was glad to see the back of him. It wasn't that she had anything against him personally. He was probably a very nice man. But she had been messed around in hospital for far too long. And certainly the treatment hadn't seemed to help all that much. In fact, she had begun to feel like a guinea pig, and she wasn't going to get caught up in that again. She could get better by herself. Viruses didn't live forever. At least, she didn't think they did. She would get well in her own good time. And a lot faster if her worry about Danny could only be lifted.

As soon as the door closed behind the doctor, Dominic put both his arms around her again, holding her more firmly against him and giving her very secure support. She nestled her head against his shoulder, wondering if his strength could flow into her. Certainly she was beginning to feel better with him holding her so close. She would make an effort to get going soon. But just for a moment or two...she could dream a little, couldn't she? Dream that he loved her, had always loved her, and she had come home.

"Tell me about your baby, Carrie. Tell me what the problem is. Ask me whatever it is you want me to do."

The words were spoken in a curiously flat manner, totally neutral as far as any feeling was concerned, but Carrie could feel the warmth and the kindness behind the intent. She was a silly little fool for dreaming of more from him. One could never really go back. And the past had all been a lie, anyway, on his side. She had come for Dominic's help. He was offering it. So she would gratefully accept it. Then go.

Carrie took a deep steadying breath and began her story at the beginning of the problem. She had been sick. Someone had rung for an ambulance. She omitted to tell Dominic that it was Danny who was so concerned for her that he had rung for help. That was irrelevant to the problem. Everything had worked fine until they got to the hospital. The authorities there had found out Danny didn't have anyone to look after him.

She was too newly back in the country to have any friends or acquaintances she could trust. Her parents were both dead, and any family relationships that still existed had all been estranged when her mother and stepfather had married. She didn't even know where they were. So the welfare people had been called in to look after Danny.

At first she had been intensely grateful. The problem had developed later. She had signed herself out of hospital when it was obvious that they weren't doing anything more for her. Then she wanted Danny back. The welfare people refused point-blank. They said she wasn't well enough to look after a child. Which was, in her opinion, totally unjustified. They had no right to keep a child from his own mother.

"You don't think they might have a point?" Dominic's voice was filled with dry sarcasm.

"I would have coped," Carrie replied defensively. "I always do. After all, I got to you, didn't I?"

"Only just."

"But I did it."

"Yes," he said heavily. "You did it."

"And looking after Danny wouldn't be nearly as much effort. He's never any trouble. He's the best child in the world. And I want him back. He'll be fretting for me, not knowing what's going on. He probably feels unloved. Strangers won't give him the kind of attention I do, and nothing will be familiar to him like in Fiji...."

"Fiji?"

"That's where we came from. What he's used to. He could be psychologically scarred in an institution over here with everything unfamiliar to him. He needs me. It's wrong to separate a child from his mother. I have to have him back, Dominic."

She lifted her head, wanting to make her appeal straight to his face. Her eyes pleaded her case as eloquently as they could. "All I'm asking is that you make one or two little phone calls. To the right people. To cut through the red tape. The small-minded rules and regulations. To get Danny back with me where he belongs." She searched his eyes anxiously, pleadingly. "Will you do that for me, Dominic?"

He slowly nodded his assent. "Yes, I'll do that for you, Carrie."

A feeling of wild triumph overtook Carrie. She had succeeded. Against all the odds. Her head dizzied with delight. She leaned it on Dominic's shoulder, just for a few moments. He couldn't know what it meant to her. She would be gone soon. Out of his life again. But Danny would be coming back into hers. It was enough. She felt a new burst of purpose surging through her body. I'll get better quickly now, she promised herself.

"Thank you," she murmured in heartfelt relief, and nearly added, "that makes up for all the pain you've ever caused me," but that would be a mistake. She must never confess the agony of mind and heart that Dominic Savage had given her. That was too long ago. Instead she said, "I'll always remember you for doing this." She would anyway. There was no lie in that.

"But first, I'm taking you home, Carrie."

The grateful glow was instantly dispelled by a wave of horror. Oh, no, she thought, not that! She couldn't allow Dominic back into her life. That would be a road to disaster. Maybe worse than what she already had. He would reopen wounds and make more. And he would see where she lived, and that alone would be too dreadful. And... and... somehow she had to put a stop to this idea immediately.

"You can't do that!" she cried in alarm, lifting her head to assert herself again. His face had an even more determined look than before, and the blue eyes blazed with immutable resolution. But Carrie would not be shaken from the course she had to take. "All I want from you is a little telephone call," she insisted. "Nothing more."

"If you want that telephone call to be successful, Carrie, I need the facts. All of them," he stated grimly.

Then, while she was still frantically trying to see a way around that argument, he scooped her legs off the floor and she found herself cradled firmly against his chest.

"No! No!" she protested, panicking at having control taken out of her hands. "Put me down, Dominic!" An idea came. Any evasive tactic was justified. "You can't take me home. Not today."

There was a chilled pause. His eyes gathered suspicion. "Why not, Carrie?"

"Your whole afternoon is booked with appointments. You're a busy man. You can't let those people down."

She had him there, Carrie thought triumphantly. Apparently she knew the facts about him better than he did himself. It was lucky she could remind him. He had to let her go. So near and yet so far, she thought with painful regret. But she couldn't accept his help if he meant to pursue her problem beyond what she'd asked of him.

"I'll look after that," he said grimly, and began striding to the door, holding her tightly clamped to him. She couldn't even struggle against the grip he had on her.

"You can't carry me like this," she cried in desperation.

"Yes, I can."

"I'm too heavy," she pleaded.

His eyes raked hers in challenging disbelief. "You're lighter than an armful of fairy floss. And something has to be done about that whether you like it or not! You want that telephone call to be successful, don't you?"

"Yes."

"Then we have to give ourselves every chance."

"But..."

"No buts! Every chance! Remember that!"

Her head whirled with frightening uncertainties. This wasn't what she had planned at all. She couldn't let Dominic go so far. The risk of terrible trouble was too high. Far too high! But how to stop him?

CHAPTER THREE

DOMINIC OPENED THE OFFICE door while Carrie was still churning over how to change his mind. He walked out of the office, then paused as his secretary's desk. Mrs. Coombe's eyebrows flew to the top of her head.

"Cancel all my appointments for this afternoon, please, Mrs. Coombe."

"Yes, Mr. Savage." It was amazing Mrs. Coombe got the words out, her jaw had dropped so far.

Carrie's last glimpse of the dragon was her look of suspended disbelief. Her whole face was frozen like a cartoon, her eyebrows near her hairline, her chin sagging down near her bosom. She was obviously shocked right out of her orderly officious mind.

Although Dominic's action was not what she wanted, Carrie had to admit to a little stab of satisfaction that it was the formidable secretary who had got her comeuppance, and not her. Next time, although, of course, there wouldn't be a next time for her, Carrie suspected that a visitor such as herself would not be subjected to red tape and officious delays. The dragon had better believe it when someone said it was urgent.

Dominic was hurtling down the corridor to the reception area. Carrie got her mind into gear. She could not allow this to go any farther. In fact, it was paramount that it be stopped forthwith.

That was easier decided than done. Dominic was a difficult force to be reckoned with now that he had the bit between his teeth. It really wasn't fair that he was so strong and she was so weak. She only had her wits to fight him with, and for some reason her wits seemed to be slowing down. Before she had managed to gather them into an offensive weapon Dominic had her at the elevators.

"Call down to the car park," he said to the receptionist. "Tell them to have my car ready for me. Immediately. I don't want to be kept waiting."

"Yes, Mr. Savage," the woman answered, her eyes goggling at the vision of her boss carrying off a woman like a latter-day pirate.

"Dominic, you must let me go," Carrie hissed at him. "What will people think?"

"I couldn't care less."

Carrie could hardly credit such an irresponsible attitude. As it was, gossip about this extraordinary incident would be rife among his employees. If he persisted in taking her home, it would make it ten times worse. She had to be more insistent, not only for her own sake, but for his, as well.

"Think of your wife!" she whispered urgently.

His face underwent an almost violent change. Hostility, anger, a rage of intense frustration blazed down at her. "That's precisely whom I am thinking of," he rasped, the blue eyes as bitter as a winter storm and total disapproval spiking through every word.

Carrie instantly shrank inside herself. If he was using her as a weapon to hurt or get back at his wife in some way, she wanted no part in his schemes. She wished she hadn't brought the subject up. Of course, he had married that girl—Alyson Hawthorn, the Super-Sophisticate and Bitch Extraordinaire. It was always going to happen. Alyson had not only told her so, but had left Carrie in no doubt about the nature of their proposed marriage.

It was obviously a marriage that wasn't wearing too well with Dominic at the moment. Carrie had never understood the kind of relationship that accepted flings on the side, but she had been forced to believe it. She remembered Alyson's derisive laughter at the idea of being offended that Dominic had slept with Carrie. "We all do it," she had said, as if it was nothing at all, and her eyes had mocked Carrie's naïveté.

She looked at Dominic, unable to conceal the pain in her eyes. "I'm sorry," she whispered. "I shouldn't have said that."

"Best to get it out in the open," he muttered irritably.

Carrie sank into deeper misery. I was right never to go back, she thought, never to see him again, never to make any contact at all. That's one decision I can be proud of. But today's decision had been a bad error of judgement, despite her own and Danny's need. The high-risk factor was getting riskier by the moment. Somehow she had to stop this right now, before everything got out of hand.

"Please... I'd rather you call me a taxi," she begged.

"The facts, Carrie. I need the facts," he reminded her.

The elevator doors opened, and Dominic had her closed into the small compartment with him and whizzing downwards before her frantic mind could produce a solid protest.

"This isn't what I planned," Carrie protested vehemently.

"Will you stop making objections?"

"I didn't mean for you to go to all this trouble."

"I can see that."

He bestowed a stern look on her that gave Carrie an odd quivery feeling in her heart. She had the distinct suspicion that when Dominic Savage made up his mind about something, not even a full-scale battle would deter him from seeing it through. It must come from being in charge of APIC, she thought. He hadn't been at all imperious when she had known him before. But she wasn't one of his employees he could order around at will.

"You can't do what you like with me, Dominic," she warned him. "I'm a free agent, you know."

"You've obviously become doggedly and impossibly independent, Carrie. But you did ask for my help. That's what you came for, and that's what you're getting."

"Only to get past the bureaucrats."

"I have to know the relevant facts in order to achieve that," he said with grim patience.

The elevator doors opened. Dominic started moving again. There were people eagerly offering assistance, a Daimler waiting with its front doors open and its engine humming at a low thrum. Carrie was lowered onto a cold leather seat, and Dominic's arms slid away from her.

"All right?" he asked softly.

Reluctantly, wearily, she lifted her eyes, feeling raw and very vulnerable as she met the sharp concern in his. "I made a mistake, Dominic," she said flatly.

"Please . . . just forget I ever came. Forget everything I said. I'll manage without your help."

His mouth thinned. He pulled the seat belt across her and pressed the buckle into its slot. Then his eyes met hers again, and somehow her own feelings seemed to be reflected in their dark blue depths. "It's too late for that, Carrie," he said quietly.

Then he shut the door on her and quickly rounded the car to the driver's side. Someone was holding his door open, then closed it after him as Dominic settled on the seat beside her and fastened his own safety belt. One hand gripped the steering wheel, the other curled around the gearshift. He didn't look at her again. He simply said, "Tell me where you live, Carrie."

A trip home, she silently resolved, and that's all. She would definitely dismiss him then. It was bad enough having to put up with him taking her home this one day. She would have nothing more to do with him. Ever! Her anxiety over Danny, and her sickness, had obviously dulled her brain this morning. But this was where solid common sense took over.

"Ashfield," she answered tersely. "Eleven Bond Street."

The Daimler purred forward. All the luxury fittings of the car screamed money. But then everything about Dominic had always screamed money. She had been so flattered, so excited, so awed, almost, when he seemed to return her own mad attraction to him on that holiday so long ago. A brief summer madness it was, not grounded in reality at all. It had come to a brutal end when reality had caught up with her in the form of Alyson Hawthorn. And Dominic's other high-living friends.

It all came down to money, Carrie thought bitterly. Like this car. Like Alyson Hawthorn, who was another symbol of status and class, with her high connections in the gentocracy, or whatever it was called. The people with old money. They inevitably intermarried. That was the way the world was made to move. Carrie had recognised that even then. The same reality was just as brutal now.

The drive to Ashfield seemed to take forever, although it could only have been twenty minutes or so. The feeling of strain and tension in the car made light conversation impossible. Besides, they really had nothing to say to each other. They came from different worlds, occupied different worlds, and Carrie spent the time wretchedly castigating herself for being such a fool as to invite even the briefest connection between them.

They turned into Bond Street. The tenements had been built late in the last century—dingy, squalid semidetached houses planned for manual workers who did not need light or sunshine or hope in their lives, only a hand-to-mouth existence with a roof over their heads. Carrie saw Dominic Savage's mouth grimace in distaste. In his life, he rarely had to face such grim relics of the labouring class, Carrie thought. It was so different to what he was used to. She had known he would disapprove of the kind of home she could afford.

He parked in front of the entrance. Carrie managed to get out of the car before Dominic could get to her to help. It was most important that she assert her independence as quickly as possibly and get on with her life without him.

"Which flat is it?" he asked.

Number 11 was a three-storey tenement, and Dominic had his head tilted, looking at the top storey.

"It's the basement flat," Carrie answered. "Down these steps."

She hurried ahead, quickly grasping the thin railing of the rusty cast-iron fence that lined the stairway to keep herself steady.

"Let me help you."

"No, Dominic. I'm all right now."

He caught up with her and took her arm anyway as she bolted down the steps. She didn't bother protesting. She kept her gaze averted from him, not wanting to see his face. No dreaming now. Stupid to have indulged herself even for a few moments. She knew only too well what his expression would reflect.

The tiny porch in front of the door seemed hopelessly crowded with him standing next to her. Carrie snatched the key out of her handbag, jammed it into the lock and opened the door. She stepped into the hallway and switched on the light. Even in the daytime that was necessary.

She didn't try to stop Dominic from coming in. Give him his way now, Carrie thought fiercely, then refuse anything he suggests. Refuse point-blank. That would get rid of him.

He followed her to the kitchen at the back, pausing momentarily to look into the single bedroom and cast his eyes around the cluttered living room. He muttered something under his breath that sounded distinctly like an appalled oath, but Carrie determinedly ignored it.

"Well, this is home!" she said with forced cheer. "And now that you've got me here, you've discharged any sense of duty you were feeling. Thank you for your kindness and consideration, and—"

"Carrie, this is dreadful!" he cut in, his brow furrowed with concern, his eyes stabbing her with their total rejection of her definition of "home," his face set in an even grimmer mould of disapproval.

"You shouldn't say things like that," she reprimanded with stiff pride. "Even if you do mean them."

"This is no place to bring up a baby," he said in a softer tone.

"We cope," she said defensively. "We always have and always will."

His expression slowly changed into a more disturbing one. Carrie told herself she had to be mistaken, but he seemed to be looking at her with an intensely hungry yearning, as though she had something he wanted very much. Her spine prickled with danger warnings. She eyed him warily, afraid that he was going to spring something on her that she wouldn't like at all.

"In your condition," he continued softly, "and in this place, I can understand what the welfare people think. They believe they're doing the child a favour—"

"They're not!"

"Don't interrupt, Carrie. Open your mind to the problems they see. That I see. It's quite obvious to me what is needed if you want your baby back. If you want the best chance of getting him and keeping him. What we have to do is present them with a different situation. One where no doubts about your welfare can arise—"

"What are you suggesting?" Carrie leapt in, the worst suspicions forming in her mind.

"I have a large home with live-in staff. Plenty of space for you and Danny. I want you to come home with me now, Carrie. We'll get things organized for Danny, and then I'll have the strongest possible case to present to the welfare people. You'll have your baby back tomorrow. I promise you that."

Carrie stared at him blank-eyed as her mind whirled in horror at his scheme. She had suspected something, but not this! What did he think he was doing? Setting up a ménage à trois with her and his wife? Was he trying to get at Alyson, teach her a lesson? Was Alyson playing around too much and not giving Dominic what he wanted? Carrie recalled his reaction when she had first spoken of her baby. Was Alyson refusing to give him children?

But bringing a former lover into his home! No way could Carrie be a party to that! The very thought curled her toes with revulsion. She sat down on the wooden stool in the kitchen, suddenly feeling quite ill again. She shook her head in an attempt to clear it.

"No, Dominic," she said very firmly. "Thank you, but no. I won't do it."

"Carrie, you're not thinking straight," he argued. "If you refuse, it might mean more delay in getting Danny back."

"I won't do it," she said, her eyes fiercely defying and denying the persuasive appeal.

It wasn't even a dilemma. For her and Danny to be placed in the situation that Dominic proposed would be even worse than the situation they were in now. And if he got even a hint of how matters really lay, it could lead to the dislocation of so many people's lives. She had no choice. No choice at all. No matter how much hurt and anguish it caused her, she had to refuse the treacherous option that Dominic was holding out to her.

"Carrie, you're not being reasonable," Dominic pressed. "It must be because you've been so sick..."

Funny how people could distort their lives and twist things up. She had never understood the values by which he and Alyson lived, but this was truly warped.

"I'll never change my mind. Not about that," she repeated for emphasis.

There was a nerve-tearing pause, then very quietly he put the question, "What did I do that was so wrong, Carrie?"

It trapped her into looking up, and she was momentarily caught in that black empty place in the past—the time when she had turned her back on his kind of life and walked away with desolation in her heart. Her own pain seemed to be reflected in his eyes, yet he couldn't be thinking of that. Her walking away couldn't have hurt him. Not really. Only perhaps his male ego. For a little while. And, of course, he always had Alyson to help him forget.

Besides, he couldn't be talking about that. He was referring to today's encounter. She was messing up his plan. "It's just wrong for me, Dominic," she said flatly.

"Do you hate me so much?" he asked, each word slowly enunciated like the clap of doom.

Dominic really did have everything distorted, Carrie thought sadly. He had so many good points, and her feelings towards him were the very opposite to hate. If only... but she wasn't going to start on if onlys again. Reality had to be faced, however brutal it was. She managed a wry little smile.

"I don't hate anybody, Dominic. Particularly not you."

"I see," he muttered, but he didn't seem to see anything at all. His eyes had a glazed look as though they were focused inward.

"I'll find another way around the problem," she said dully. Perhaps she would leave Sydney and find a place in the country. Taree, Dubbo...any large country town might offer some form of work that was in her line of training. Perhaps a pastry cook at a bakery. Or in a homemade pie shop. She didn't have to be a chef. And living would be cheaper out of the city. If she could get a job...

"I'll find another way, too," Dominic said in a tone of strong resolution.

She frowned at him. "Please let it go. All I wanted was a telephone call—"

"I'll do that."

"—nothing else."

"Leave it to me."

Carrie didn't know whether he meant it or not, but she couldn't take any more from him. "Goodbye, Dominic," she said flatly.

His eyes locked on hers for a long tense moment, then slowly he nodded. "I'll let myself out."

"Thank you," Carrie whispered, her voice choked by a huge lump of suppressed emotion in her throat.

"Goodbye, Carrie."

The way he said it was almost a caress. Tears pricked at her eyes. He was going...out of her life forever this time. She heard his footsteps receding down the hallway, heard the front door open and shut quietly behind him. For a long while Carrie sat totally immobile, her face white, her body lifeless. Then for the first time in many years, she buried her head in her arms on the kitchen counter and sobbed bitterly into her loneliness.

CHAPTER FOUR

YESTERDAY HAD BEEN more weakening than Carrie had expected. She felt limp, drained, without purpose, will or energy. She berated herself for letting this happen to her. She could not rely on Dominic Savage for anything. She had to pull herself together. And the first thing she had to do was start eating more, even if she had to force food down her throat. Then maybe she would have the energy to get herself better organized instead of trying to think of some easy way out of her problem.

She cooked herself some scrambled eggs and managed to consume a piece of toast with them. Then she made coffee with milk. It was a bit rich for her taste but she drank it, determined to put weight on any way she could. She had been existing on soup lately, not wanting anything more than that. But obviously it was not enough.

In fact, if she had remembered to have some lunch yesterday before setting out to see Dominic, she might have fared a lot better instead of succumbing to that awful weakness. Today she would set herself a proper diet and follow it rigidly, no matter whether she felt like it or not. If those welfare people thought she was suffering from malnutrition she would soon set them straight.

The thought came to her that she could ring or write to her member of parliament. It was a pity she hadn't registered herself on the electoral role as soon as she had come back from Fiji, but it was the kind of official duty that everyone let slip until a looming election served as a reminder. She would see to it today. Then she could proceed along that line, even though it meant more red tape.

She washed up the few things she'd used, fired with new purpose to get going and achieve something. She did feel better for having made herself eat a more substantial meal than she had become accustomed to. As she went to her bedroom to dress, she couldn't help looking at the flat through Dominic's eyes.

He was right in one respect. This was no place to bring up a child. It compared so badly to the sun-filled *bure* that she and Danny had occupied in Fiji. This was nothing but a dingy little hole in the ground. When she had first occupied it, it had been filthy with old grime. She had scrubbed and cleaned, even fumigated the place. However, the only difference now was that it was a clean dingy hole instead of a dirty one. Even the bright curtains she had put up did not make up for the lack of sunlight.

She had to move. Her ambition to be a chef in a top restaurant was not as important as having the right kind of place for bringing up her son. She knew Danny hated the flat as much as she did, although he had never grumbled or complained about it. He had accepted her insistence that it was just a temporary place until she had a permanent position. But that kind of position was not easy to get in Sydney, Carrie had found, despite her excellent references and years of experience. A country town was better anyway,

Carrie decided. It would get her right away from Dominic Savage.

Having made up her mind on a new course of action, Carrie got herself moving. She put on a brightly flowered skirt to cheer herself up. It had an elasticised waist so she didn't have to worry about it falling off. The matching T-shirt with the hibiscus-flower motif looked very baggy on her but she tucked it in, then bloused out the looseness so that it didn't look too bad. At least she could wear her flat comfortable Roman sandals today, so walking shouldn't be too much of a problem.

She made her way to the electoral office at Ashfield and registered herself as a voter. Next she bought a writing pad and envelopes. She also purchased a newspaper to read advertisements for jobs up the country. At the very last moment she remembered food. The tomatoes looked good at the fruit shop. She bought some salad things. That was healthy. She also stopped at a bakery shop and bought a custard tart. It would help put weight on.

Despite her good breakfast, Carrie's burst of energy was fading fast. On her way home she rested in the park for an hour or two. She felt a bit too dizzy to read the newspaper. Focussing on little print seemed to make things worse. She could do that later, Carrie decided, when she felt better. She watched the birds as they wheeled and soared, free and unhindered by any welfare people or red tape. They twittered happily between themselves. Life was good. And so it would be for her and Danny again, once they were back together.

After a while, Carrie remembered the custard tart and ate it. Birds swooped down to pick up the crumbs.

She smiled at their antics, pleased to be passing the time so pleasantly. She wondered if Danny was pleased with anything, wherever he was living. She hoped so. She hoped he wasn't too miserable. Soon, she silently promised him. I'll get you back soon, my little love.

It was midafternoon by the time she returned to Bond Street. The first thing she saw was a Daimler parked outside number 11. She halted dead in her tracks, her heart palpitating at an alarming rate. "Oh, hell!" she thought. "What is Dominic up to now?"

Then she remembered the telephone call he had said he would make, and the thought that he might have brought news of Danny had her feet instantly scurrying forward.

He didn't hear her coming. He was sitting on the basement steps, irritably throwing small pebbles at some invisible mark on the wall. His brow was furrowed. Despite his maturity and the superbly tailored business suit he wore, he looked like a petulant little boy who had lost his favourite lolly. Carrie's heart did a funny little flip. But it was no good thinking of him like . . . like she might think of Danny. No good feeling anything for Dominic Savage. That was forbidden territory.

"Hello, there!" she called out brightly. "I hope I haven't kept you waiting too long."

The frown instantly disappeared. He rose eagerly to his feet, but when he turned to her his face had assumed a guarded look, the blue eyes wary and watchful. "No," he said. "I've had a fair bit to do. The appointments from yesterday afternoon."

"Of course." She flushed. "But that wasn't really my fault. I did—"

"I appreciate that, Carrie," he cut in quickly.

Her eyes searched his anxiously, hopefully. "Have you found out anything from the welfare people?"

"Yes."

She looked at him in expectant appeal.

He gestured towards the door. "May we go inside?"

"Oh! All right." She hurried forward, ready to agree to almost anything just to hear about Danny. Any news was better than no news at all.

"Let me carry your parcels."

She handed them over reluctantly, but they were getting heavy and she needed her hands free to get out her key anyway.

"Have you been overdoing it again?" Dominic asked sternly.

"Don't fuss. I'm fine," she insisted, although his presence did make her feel a bit shaky and feverish. She probably needed to sit down. Not so close to him. When she was close to him the memories were all too sharp, and she couldn't afford them. Not if she was to remain sane and sensible.

She quickly unlocked the door and led him to the kitchen. He placed the plastic bags on the counter and sat down on Danny's stool, on the living room side of the kitchen counter. He looked as if he meant to stay for some time, and Carrie couldn't exactly dismiss him. At least, not straight away.

"Would you like a cup of tea? Or coffee?" she asked, driven to be polite in her need to know about Danny.

His serious face cracked into a slight smile. "Thank you. I would."

"Which one?"

"Whatever you're having."

"Tea."

"Fine."

Carrie put the kettle on to boil, then sat down on her stool, facing him across the counter. "Well?" she pleaded, unable to wait any longer.

A wave of resolution passed over his face. "Danny will be coming back tomorrow."

Carrie had not been aware of how tensely wound up she was until that firm pronouncement hit her and she let out all the tightness in a shuddering sigh. A well of jubilation flooded her mind. A spring of happiness bubbled through her body. She wanted to leap off her stool, to hug Dominic Savage, to kiss him, to thank him, to show her gratitude. All of which was impossible.

"I'll never be able to repay you," she said feelingly. "To say thank you simply does not express—"

"There is one proviso."

Carrie stopped in full flight. Her stomach turned over. He couldn't be returning to his proposal of yesterday. He just couldn't! She had been so definite in her rejection of it. If he was trying to blackmail her... Surely Dominic could not stoop so low, no matter how pressed he felt to achieve his purpose. Whatever that was.

She stood up, too agitated to remain seated. The blood rushed from her face, but the light of bitter battle was in her green eyes. "What proviso is that?" she demanded icily.

Dominic rose from his stool, his expression clearly indicating that he was prepared to do battle. "Don't look at me like that, Carrie," he shot at her. "It's not what you think. I'm not double-crossing you. This is genuine concern for you and your baby," he insisted vehemently, then tempered his tone to a more reasoning note as he added, "please hear me out. For your own sake. And the child's."

"I'm not going to your home, Dominic," she fired at him. "I don't care what you say or how you twist it. I'm not going!"

His face tightened. "You made that abundantly clear yesterday."

"Then what is this proviso?" Carrie demanded tersely, every atom of her being poised to explode in fiery rebellion.

Dominic's chest rose and fell as he administered a deep breath to his lungs. He made a visible effort to relax, to speak calmly so as not to upset her. "Your accommodation here. It is a stumbling block, Carrie. Truly it is."

"Then what are you suggesting?" Her eyes flared a hot warning.

Dominic did not flinch. He held her gaze steadily, projecting calm reassurance. "My company owns an apartment. We use it for interstate executives, business associates, overseas clients . . . people we want to accommodate who prefer not to stay in a hotel. And with the way property values are moving, it's a good investment. It's more appropriate housing for you than here, Carrie. You and Danny could use it until such time as—"

"And put myself further in your debt?" she flashed at him, a fierce pride putting a sharp edge on every word.

"Not at all. There's no reason you shouldn't use it. Until you're better."

"While your company is inconvenienced by not having ready accommodation for your executives, associates and clients," she sliced back sarcastically.

Dominic grimaced, shook his head as though in some pain, then tried again, slowly and patiently. "At the present moment, the apartment is being redecorated. It's already been cleared of most of its furniture, leaving only the barest basics. If you can put up with the nuisance of an interior decorator coming and going, and doing things around you, at least you will be in better living quarters than this place can offer. It's spacious, with well-appointed bathrooms and kitchen. And lots of windows to let in the light."

Carrie was tempted, despite her suspicions. "This is a genuine offer, Dominic?" she asked. "I won't accept charity. I can always pay—"

"Carrie, I've explained it all to you. Our company doesn't really need your money. The apartment is not expected to earn an income. That's not its purpose. What more can I say?" he replied with every appearance of earnest sincerity. "The main point is, the welfare people approve of the plan. They'll release Danny tomorrow. If you agree."

She was plunged into a quandary. It was an opportunity too good to miss, yet if it meant a continued association with Dominic... If he had some problem with his marriage, she didn't want to get involved in it. In fact, she couldn't really afford any involvement with him at all. There was always Danny to consider, apart from her own disturbing feelings.

Some of her agony of mind shadowed her eyes. "I don't want you . . . coming to see me, Dominic."

The relief on his face seemed to make nonsense of all her thoughts on the matter. Apparently he didn't want to see her. Had she got everything wrong? Or had he changed his mind since yesterday, realising that it was totally unfair to use her need as a means to settle his own?

"Only if it's necessary," he said, obviously anxious to reassure her.

Maybe he felt guilty for what he had formerly proposed. And she had always thought Dominic kind and generous by nature, even though some of his morals didn't bear too much inspection. She hesitated for a while, tossing alternatives around in her mind. Her need to be reunited with Danny won out.

"All right. I accept."

"Thank God!" Dominic breathed, his relief becoming even more pronounced. "You're being reasonable for once. I'll go and bring the suitcases in."

He had turned away when Carrie was struck by a hornet's nest of uncertainty. "You expected me to accept, Dominic?"

He swung back, ready to appease again. "It was the only sensible decision to make, Carrie." He gave her a wry little smile. "But I must confess I wasn't at all certain you'd make it. I brought suitcases just in case, so to speak."

"I see," she said, trying to quell the nervous flutters in her stomach. She had the feeling that she had just crossed a line that wasn't as straight as she would have liked it to be. But Danny was on the other side of it, and her yearning for him could not be denied. "Thank you, Dominic," she said, not very firmly.

"It will be all right, Carrie," he assured her. "I promise you."

She trailed after him as far as the bedroom door. At least she hadn't been here long enough to gather much stuff, she thought, so the packing wouldn't take long. She had given away all unnecessary belongings before leaving Fiji.

She sat down on the bed, feeling weak from the stress of being with Dominic. But after tomorrow she wouldn't see him again, unless it was necessary. Which it wouldn't be. She could cope with everything. If this company apartment didn't work out, she could always leave. Once she had Danny back. And once she was well, she would get a job in the country. This was only a temporary measure, and it would stay a temporary measure.

Dominic came in with two large suitcases and set them open on Danny's bed. He opened the top drawer of the chest near the bed and began scooping clothes out.

Carrie gaped at him. "What are you doing?" she asked, shocked that he would take such a liberty. "They're my underclothes!"

"I thought I'd help you pack," he said matter-of-factly.

Blood had rushed to Carrie's face. "No, you won't!"

"Why not? You look as if you need a rest, Carrie. I've done this plenty of times for my wife—"

Mention of his wife tipped Carrie into a maelstrom of violent emotion. "I don't want you touching my underclothes!" she cried vehemently.

He gave her a look that told her he remembered touching far more intimate things than her underclothes. Carrie burned. Her heart pounded a frantic protest. She told herself it was the humiliation of it all, but she knew it was more than that. She was just too frightened to examine what she was really feeling. It was far too dangerous to her sense of rightness.

"That was eight years and two months ago," she stated tightly, trying her utmost to get in control of herself. "Before you married!"

"Yes. I remember," he answered softly, and there was something infinitely disquieting in the vivid blue eyes. Again that look of haunted, raw, naked pain crossed his face.

"Things have changed," Carrie said, flustered. "I've changed. You've changed. And I don't want... I don't want..." She lifted her hands helplessly, unable to hold the gaze that remembered too many things that had to be forgotten. And stay forgotten!

"May I pack food from the kitchen?" he asked quietly.

Carrie could feel the tension flooding from him in waves. She nodded, too choked to speak.

"Then I'll go and get boxes out of the car."

Carrie got up to pack. She was trembling so much she had to sit down again. But when she heard Dominic returning with the boxes, she forced her legs to hold her and moved to the chest of drawers, determined to start the packing. And finish it. At least in the bedroom.

Dominic brought her a cup of tea. She had completely forgotten that she had put the kettle on to boil. She thanked him abruptly, and he did not linger with her. She instantly regretted the abruptness. It had been kind of him. But she couldn't allow herself to go soft. If she gave him an inch, she had a dreadful suspicion that he might take the inevitable mile.

He took boxes out to the car while she slowly filled the suitcases. She had almost finished when he stopped in the bedroom doorway.

"What about the furniture, Carrie? Is it yours?"

"No. Only the curtains."

"I'll take them down for you and put them in a box, too," he said. "I've cleared the kitchen and the laundry at the back. Is it all right if I do the bathroom?" he asked tactfully, aware that it could be personal to her.

"I'll do that," she said.

"Okay," he agreed, and briskly collected her cup and saucer before disappearing again.

When Carrie finally went to inspect what he'd done, she found he had been amazingly efficient. Everything had been tidied as he had packed, and he had left nothing behind except what belonged in the flat. The whole place was as spick-and-span as she would have left it. She looked at him in questioning amazement.

"I am house trained," he said dryly. "I even cook when called upon."

Heaven above, she thought, he has changed! The old Dominic she had known would have had no more idea about cooking than the man in the moon!

"Thank you again for all your help, Dominic," she said stiffly, doing her best to let him know she would not be calling upon him for anything more.

He made a dismissive gesture. "Are you ready to go now?"

"Yes."

She locked the flat and they drove to the real estate agent that handled the rental. Dominic insisted that Carrie remain in the car and rest while he handed over the key and finalised matters. She did not argue. She felt exhausted, mentally, emotionally and physically.

She realised after a while that she hadn't asked Dominic where the company's apartment was, but then decided it didn't really matter. So long as the welfare people accepted it as suitable for Danny. That was all that counted.

CHAPTER FIVE

WHEN THEY GOT GOING AGAIN, Dominic headed the Daimler into the city. Carrie closed her eyes. It was easier to shut out Dominic's presence if she couldn't see him. Besides, she was very tired. It had been a more active day than she'd had for some time. An extremely wearing day.

"Carrie?"

She didn't really want to respond to the soft call of her name. Her body did, completely without her volition. The tone he used, the caring it implied... Little quivers fluttered through her stomach. She should never have gone to him. It was all coming back. Not just a memory any more. Raw reality. But it would be over soon, she told herself. Meanwhile, politeness demanded a reply. "Yes?" she asked wearily.

"There wasn't any baby food stocked in the kitchen cupboards." There was a puzzled note in his voice. "And what about a bassinet or a cot? If you're sleeping with the baby, you won't get your proper rest," he added in anxious concern.

Carrie heaved a deep sigh to relieve the tension that instantly tore at her nerves. He had to know the truth now. At least, as much of the truth as he needed to know. After all, he would be meeting Danny tomorrow. Carrie concentrated on injecting a matter-of-fact tone into her voice.

"I'm sorry, Dominic. I may have misled you just a little bit. I think of Danny as my baby. He is. But he's not exactly a tiny cuddly thing any more. He's a real little boy. He eats what I eat. And that was his bed you put the suitcases on."

"Oh!" It was the sound of relief. "That's all right, then. A bed," he added, as though to himself, and as if it was a matter of some importance.

To Carrie's relief, that ended the conversation. Of course, it was bound to be resumed tomorrow, after Dominic met Danny, and she had to get herself mentally prepared for it. But there was time enough to think about that. Once over that hurdle she was home free. If everything went right.

Once they were in the inner city, Carrie snapped alert again. She wondered if Dominic was returning to his office for some reason, but they passed Bridge Street and went right down to Circular Quay, turning into the basement car park of an ultra-modern skyscraper that stood on the waterfront of the harbour.

It made sense when Carrie stopped to think about it. APIC would naturally want their important clients or associates placed at the hub of things and in a prestigious area. Harbour frontage was always prestigious. The welfare people couldn't possibly look down their noses at this address!

Dominic wouldn't let Carrie lift anything from the car. He hefted the two large suitcases over to the elevators. He used a slot key to open the doors of one elevator and quickly ushered Carrie inside, following her with the packed bags.

"I hope you're not nervous of heights, Carrie," he said anxiously, as the lift started upwards.

"Not at all," she assured him.

Again he looked relieved. "All the glass in the apartment is laminated and break-proof, and the whole place is air-conditioned. So it's completely safe. I'm sorry it isn't comfortably furnished as yet, but it will be, bit by bit."

"It'll be fine, Dominic. Anything will be fine as long as it means..."

"You get Danny back," he finished for her, giving her a smile of intimate understanding that took Carrie's breath away.

For several rocky moments, it was as if there had been no eight years and two months. They were sharing together, just as they did before his friends had come and Alyson had put a different face on their relationship. Then Carrie wrenched her gaze from his and stared at the doors, willing the elevator to stop, willing the doors to open, urgently needing to escape the intimacy Dominic had evoked. Endless seconds ticked over. She felt her nerves stretch to snapping point before the elevator cooperated with her frantic willing and came to a halt.

The doors opened and she stepped out, concentrating fiercely on her new surroundings, doing her utmost to shut Dominic out of her mind. Her body was a weak mess, but at least she could control her mind. She had to, or she would never get through this ordeal.

The private lobby that led into the apartment was tiled to an old Etruscan pattern. Reluctantly but determinedly, she followed Dominic into an enormous living room, carpeted in off white, which would be a nightmare to keep clean, Carrie thought. In fact, it must have been recently cleaned, because it looked as good as new. The only furniture was two blue-grey leather armchairs and a Travertine coffee table, all of which looked vaguely familiar to Carrie. Were they duplicates of the ones in Dominic's office?

She dismissed the thought as her attention was pleasantly distracted by the magnificent view of Sydney Harbour from the floor-to-ceiling windows. "How high up are we?" she asked.

"Um...nineteenth floor, I think. The elevator is private, so you'll have no trouble coming and going, Carrie. It's only a short distance from the Botanical Gardens, so you'll be able to take Danny for walks. There are shops along the quay...."

"You business people really do yourself proud. The best of everything!" Carrie remarked drily, then realising she might have given offence, she offered an apologetic smile. "This is—" she gestured towards the view "—fantastic!"

He grinned with deep pleasure. "Good! Have a look around while I bring all your things up."

Carrie steadfastly battled the effect of his grin, turning to the view as he retreated to the elevator. Her heart gradually steadied. Dominic probably grinned at everyone like that. It meant nothing personal. Not really personal. She had been difficult about coming here. Now he had won his point. That was all.

This must be what they call a penthouse apartment, Carrie thought, and could not help wondering what it cost. Probably close to a million dollars, with this view and position. Perhaps more. It was going to be an awful comedown when she had to move out, but in the meantime, she might as well enjoy the high life. It was an experience she never expected to have again.

The dining room had a large laminated table and four rather ordinary chairs that didn't suit the place at all. Perhaps it was a workplace for the interior decorator, Carrie thought, and would be replaced by an appropriate suite when the time came.

There were three bedrooms, each with its own luxurious bathroom and beautifully crafted built-in wardrobes. The master bedroom was the only one with furniture—a king-size bed, already made up, and a bedside table on which sat a portable television set.

The kitchen seemed huge and was the last word in modernity. It had a computerised microwave oven as well as double fan-forced ovens, a barbecue grill beside the burners, a dishwasher, even a garbage disposal unit. Carrie dreamed of the meals she could cook with such excellent facilities.

The laundry was spacious, with a top-brand automatic washer and matching dryer, as well as a tub and ironing facilities. Of course, living up here, there would be no pegging the washing on a clothesline, Carrie thought, bemused by another new experience for her.

She returned to the kitchen for a further exploration. There was a huge two-doored refrigerator, and when she opened the freezer side, she found it stocked with ice cream and cakes and pies and all sorts of frozen meals and snacks. Dominic came into the kitchen with a box of food from the flat. She hid the instant rise of inner tension as best she could and turned to him inquiringly.

"There's a whole lot of food in here, Dominic."

He shrugged. "Someone comes and does that. You might as well use it up, Carrie. Otherwise it will get thrown out before we install anyone else in here. Whatever is usable, use it."

She frowned. "You'd better tell whoever does it to stop doing it," she said. "Until I'm gone."

Telling herself to keep acting naturally, she opened the other door of the refrigerator. It revealed a huge stock of soft drinks and fruit juices, butter and margarine, a wide variety of cheeses and even some oranges and apples. Carrie shook her head. "I think you should take these things home with you, Dominic."

He slid her an ironic smile. "I assure you, I don't need it. In fact, if I took it home my housekeeper would think I'd gone insane and hand in her notice. Do me a favour and just use it as you please. It'd be a pity to waste it."

Amazing how rich people could just throw things away, Carrie thought with a dash of her own irony... bitter irony. She imagined they didn't think twice about it, while she had always had to think twice about everything. Except for that month with Dominic.

Carrie instantly clamped down on that treacherous memory and opened the doors to a built-in pantry. There were tins of food galore, packets of biscuits, bottles of sauces, all the basic ingredients for all sorts of cooking, spices and condiments—almost a real chef's pantry.

"Use what you like of that, as well," Dominic said carelessly. "Before it goes stale. We'll make a clean sweep of everything when the decorating's done."

It was sinful extravagance to throw it away, Carrie thought critically. "You're sure?" she asked, not wanting to take any advantage that she shouldn't, but unable to countenance such waste.

"Positive," Dominic insisted.

She sighed in relief. "I won't have to shop for weeks," she remarked, her eyes feasting on all the provisions.

"You'll need meat and fruit and vegetables," Dominic said with a disapproving frown.

"Yes. You're right," Carrie quickly agreed.

"I've brought everything up. Do you want to unpack yourself, Carrie?"

"Yes, I do. And thanks! I'm terribly grateful for all you've done, Dominic."

Either he sensed her anxiety for him to leave or he wanted to leave anyway, because he didn't press her except to say, "Promise me you'll take it in easy stages and not wear yourself out."

"I promise." She found herself giving him a smile before she could stop it, and he smiled back, unsettling her all over again.

"Okay. Come and I'll show you how the intercom works. The interior decorator will be coming in the morning and you'll have to let her in."

She steeled herself to go with him and listen to his instructions. They were easy to remember. He gave her the key then stepped into the elevator.

"I don't know what time I'll get here with Danny tomorrow afternoon, Carrie. You just take care of yourself so you'll be fine when we come. Okay?"

"I want to come with you, Dominic," Carrie pleaded, wanting to see Danny as soon as possible and also afraid of Dominic's possible reaction to her son. There were so many uncertainties about how Danny would react to Dominic, as well.

Dominic reached out and took her hands before she could stop him, his warm fingers curling around hers, sending her pulse haywire. He pressed them earnestly, as earnestly as his eyes begged her cooperation.

"Believe me, Carrie, this will all work out much more smoothly if you leave it to me. I know how to handle these people and I can do it better alone. You're sure to get emotional, Carrie, and that's not the way. Let me get your son for you. Trust me."

She couldn't doubt his sincerity. He did mean well. And maybe she had been her own worst enemy in her futile dealings with the welfare people. Dumbly she nodded her head in compliance with his plan. Trusting him, though, was a different matter. She had drunk at that well once before. The aftertaste had been bitter, and the effects had lasted a long time.

He squeezed her hands in a final reassurance. "Everything will be all right," he promised.

Carrie hoped so. She nodded, too choked by another surge of emotion to say anything. He released her hands and smiled again. The doors finally closed on his smile, releasing her from the need to keep her composure.

Only one more meeting with him, she assured herself. It would probably be the most difficult and the most testing, but she would get through it somehow. The problem was that every atom of common sense she possessed dictated that she never see him again after tomorrow, but she wanted to.

She wanted to drown in his smile, to feel his eyes caress her with soft caring, to hear his beautiful voice say anything, anything at all. Or sing to her as he used to. She wanted him to hold her again, close, lovingly...

Dominic couldn't be happy with Alyson Hawthorn.

The uncharitable thought slid into her mind, and even as Carrie tried to crush it, it gave her satisfaction in a way. The truth was, she didn't want Alyson and Dominic to be happy.

But they were married!

And it would be utter madness for her to invite any further involvement with him. No matter how unfair it was, no matter what she felt for him or what he felt with her, it had to end tomorrow! The parting of the ways had to come.

CHAPTER SIX

THE SOUND OF MOVEMENT in the kitchen woke Carrie with a start. Who could it be? An intruder? Certainly not the interior decorator, because she didn't have a key. Had Dominic come back for some reason?

Carrie looked at the clock she had placed on the bedside table. Nine-thirty. She had overslept dreadfully. Not at all like the sleeping pattern she was used to recently, where she hardly seemed to close her eyes before she was awake again. But this king-size bed was so roomy and comfortable after that sagging single bed in the flat, and the pillows had been just right. Even better than that, though, was the knowledge that Danny would be with her again today. It had removed so much stress and given her peace of mind.

Meanwhile, she had better find out who was doing what in her kitchen. Carrie slipped out of bed, donned her wraparound housecoat, tied the belt securely, then moved uneasily to the doorway.

"Is anyone out there?" she called, wanting some warning of whom she had to confront.

"Yes. I'm here."

Carrie had heard that voice before, as recently as two days ago. The dragon!

"It's me. Mrs. Coombe, dear."

Wonders will never cease, Carrie thought. I'm now "dear." I've obviously been added to Dominic Savage's list of friends and acquaintances and even granted special honours! Seeing me carried out in Dominic's arms must have really impressed the dragon.

Carrie headed for the kitchen, figuring she had better check what Dominic's secretary was up to. He hadn't given any warning about a visit from her.

Mrs. Coombe was standing over a shopping trolley, transferring parcel after parcel to the refrigerator. She glanced up as Carrie walked in. "I didn't want to wake you," she explained. "You were sleeping so peacefully."

Ah, Carrie thought, so she had been tiptoeing around, seeing what was going on. "You shouldn't have worried about it," she said. "I needed to get up. I was going shopping..."

"I've already done that for you, dear."

"What?" Carrie gaped at her, even more so when Mrs. Coombe gave her an indulgent smile.

"Yes, this is your meat here. A nice tender fillet of beef, a few sausages, a leg of lamb, some hamburger..."

Carrie was slow to recover. "Mrs. Coombe, you can't possibly... this isn't necessary."

The dragon rearranged her face into the more familiar stern look. "Mr. Savage doesn't want you wasting your strength on mundane chores."

Carrie had the mad impulse to stand at attention, salute and say, "Yes, sergeant-major." But she controlled herself and said, "This is so kind."

"Not at all. You've got to get well. I've brought a notepad and I'll put it by your bed. Anything you want, just write it down and you'll have it the same day. And, of course, you must telephone the office for anything urgent. I've put down the number you can call for a direct line to me. Any time at all. Don't hesitate."

Carrie stared in astonishment. The dragon certainly had a new appreciation of "urgent matters." Where Carrie was concerned anyway. And I'm really being pampered, she thought. It made her feel a trifle uncomfortable. Useless, really. She was so used to being self-sufficient.

"I can look after myself," she said defensively.

"I see that," Mrs. Coombe answered with a very dry look that threw Carrie into confusion. "I've brought fresh milk, and here are your vegetables and fruit," she continued with her air of competent efficiency. "If you like, I'll put them away for you. The grapes are seedless and..."

"That's enough to feed any army," Carrie protested.

"Convalescents need a lot of little delicious delicacies to tempt the appetite," Mrs. Coombe said in her no-nonsense manner. "I should know," she added in her best don't-argue-with-me voice.

Carrie felt her hand coming up to her forehead and only resisted the salute at the last moment.

The intercom rang.

"That will be the interior decorator," Carrie said distractedly. "I've got to let her in."

"Go on then," the dragon urged. "You'll have your hands full, helping with that today. I'll finish here and quietly slip away so as not to disturb you."

Carrie didn't understand how she was supposed to help, except by keeping out of the interior decorator's way, but the intercom rang again, so she didn't stop to argue. "Thank you, Mrs. Coombe."

It was a pleasant surprise to find that the interior decorator was a young woman, about the same age as Carrie, with an outgoing, friendly manner. She introduced herself as Georgina Winslow—"But please call me Gina. Everyone does"—and handed Carrie her business card. Carrie knew she had to be good at her job, despite her age. No one got to do a prestige job like this unless they were good. She suspected Dominic Savage would automatically hire the best.

And of course, the woman looked very professional, her auburn hair cut in a short chic style that suited her rather round face, which was attractive without being conventionally pretty. Her nicest feature was her bright hazel eyes. Her clothes were very smart. A cream dress printed with a geometric design in amber and brown, and a fancy leather belt that screamed designer wear.

Carrie suddenly felt extremely conscious of her unkempt appearance. "Sorry I'm not dressed...or anything. I overslept."

"That's fine. I want to look around and take some notes and measurements. Do you mind?"

"Of course not. I'll get dressed. Do you want me out of here today? Will I be in the way?"

"Oh, no!" came the quick assurance. "I'd much prefer it if you were here. People can have such different tastes. It's a lot easier if we can talk."

The strange remark left Carrie somewhat bemused. Her opinion didn't count at all. But if Gina wanted to sound out her ideas on her, Carrie didn't mind. It would be interesting to see how an interior decorator went about furnishing a place like this. And at least she didn't have to go out and perhaps miss Danny when he arrived. So this arrangement suited her admirably.

By the time she had showered, dressed and tidied herself, as well as the bedroom, Carrie found that Mrs. Coombe had gone and Gina was spreading sample books out on the dining-room table. "Would you like a cup of tea or coffee?" Carrie asked.

"Coffee, please," came the smiling response.

In the kitchen, she found that Mrs. Coombe had set out a glass of orange juice, a bowl of freshly cut fruit salad, a jug of cream and a plate of muffins that smelled as though they had been baked this morning. Tempting my convalescent appetite, Carrie thought drily. And no doubt I'll get lectured tomorrow if I don't eat everything.

She would have to stop Mrs. Coombe's visits. However kindly meant they were, Mrs. Coombe was too closely connected to Dominic Savage. Carrie made a mental note to pay him for the extra food supplies this afternoon. She would not accept charity from him. She owed him too much as it was.

Since she couldn't bear good food to be wasted, and the fruit salad was tempting, Carrie poured some cream over it and ate it while she made the coffee. Then she loaded a tray with the coffee mugs and the plate of muffins and carried it into the dining room.

"Oh, lovely!" Gina beamed at her and quickly cleared a space for the tray. "I skipped breakfast this morning and I'm starving."

"Eat as much as you like," Carrie invited.

"You must have some, too," came the quick retort. "I'll feel like a pig otherwise."

Carrie already felt full from the fruit salad but she forced down a muffin just to be companionable. Out of curiosity, she asked Gina how she set out to tackle a project such as this.

"Well, first you must know the theme the client wants. In this instance my instructions are to produce the homey touch rather than a showpiece. A place where people can really relax and feel comfortable."

That made sense, Carrie thought. If Dominic's clients preferred not to stay in hotels, they wouldn't want an impersonal atmosphere here.

"And that's where you can help me most," Gina said, looking at Carrie expectantly. "Tell me what colours you feel happy with. We don't want anything too neutral. We need warmth as well as restfulness."

"Well, I like most colours," Carrie answered, not feeling comfortable about influencing the decorating. Besides, what she said about colours was true enough. She did like most of them.

"Mr. Savage mentioned you had a little boy. What about him?"

Carrie laughed, happy at the thought that Danny would be with her in a few more hours. "Oh, he loves red and orange and yellow. He's spent most of his life in Fiji, and people in the islands seem to naturally gravitate to bright colours. It's what he's used to. But Danny is only seven years old, so what he likes won't matter."

"Sounds good to me," Gina said consideringly. "I can work with that. A lot of people like bright, cheerful colours. And red and orange and yellow are warm."

Carrie grinned. "More like hot."

Gina grinned back. "So we'll have one very hot bedroom. Let's look at fabrics and see what choice we have."

It was fun looking through the sample books and talking to Gina. The young woman seemed eager to have Carrie's opinion, so Carrie gave her preferences, but always waited until Gina had pointed out the possibilities she favoured. After all, a professional interior decorator obviously knew her job far better than Carrie did.

They were interrupted by the intercom buzzing a summons. It was a delivery man, wanting to bring up a bed. Carrie gave him entry and Gina took over, showing the man where to put it in the second bedroom. Then she asked Carrie if she could make some telephone calls.

"Now that we've chosen fabrics for this room, I'll get coordinating linen delivered for the bed so it will be ready for Danny," she explained.

Carrie felt some protest was in order. "You shouldn't really be taking any notice of what we prefer, Gina. You know, we're not permanent guests here."

Gina looked perplexed for a moment or two, and then her face brightened. "That doesn't matter. This is working out well. Let's go for broke!"

Carrie shrugged. In the end, whatever the result was, it would be Gina's responsibility. "Whatever you like," she said, secretly delighted at the thought of Danny having a nice room of his own. A bright, cheerful room. At least for a while.

She felt so happy that she went out to the kitchen to prepare a really nice lunch, hoping that Gina would share it with her. The time was passing quite easily with the young woman's company. Gina was only too pleased to accept the meal Carrie offered her.

"This is sumptuous! Really lovely! But you mustn't make a practice of feeding me." She laughed. "I don't want to end up overweight. And I don't want to be any trouble to you."

"It's no trouble," Carrie assured her. "I like doing it."

Besides, it made her feel better about using the food that had been left here. If she saved Gina some time, then she was saving Dominic time and money.

She put her individual touches to the salmon salad, and Gina enthused over the tasty dressing. "What is it? I'll buy some."

"It's my own special recipe." Then with a sense of pride and a rueful little smile, she explained, "I don't give away my secrets."

"I knew it!" Gina rolled her eyes in appreciation. "You're a professional at this, aren't you? The way you arranged the salad—the dressing, the taste! Come on, Carrie, admit it!"

Carrie laughed in pleasure, thinking how lucky she was that Gina was so appreciative. "I have had a bit of experience," she acknowledged, but wouldn't elaborate. It sounded too much like bragging to tell her about Ports o' Call, the premier restaurant at the Sheraton in Fiji, and arguably one of the finest restaurants in the world. She felt in such good spirits that it wasn't hard to eat a reasonable helping of salad herself.

The linen for Danny's bedroom arrived after lunch. The sheets and pillow slips were cream with thin lines of orange forming a geometric pattern. A vibrant orange blanket accompanied them, and there was a set of bathroom towels in exactly the same colour. Carrie made up the bed and hung the towels in the bathroom. The orange looked super there against the white and beige tiles. At least, in Carrie's opinion.

Gina seemed pleased with the effect, too. She didn't stay much longer after this, excusing herself to go hunting for the rest of the furniture for Danny's bedroom.

Her departure left Carrie at a loose end. She suddenly felt tired and decided to have a rest. It had been an eventful day, and the best event was yet to come. It wouldn't do to be feeling weak and worn out when Danny arrived.

Gina had kept her mind distracted from worrying over what was happening with Dominic and Danny, but now that Carrie was alone, with nothing to do, all sorts of possibilities presented themselves, and none of them allowed Carrie to rest easy. She kept telling herself not to cross bridges until she came to them. But there were definitely a few dangerous chasms ahead of her.

First and foremost were the feelings that Dominic aroused in her. They had to be kept under rigid control. Then there were the questions he would inevitably raise over Danny. She had been sidestepping that issue, but it couldn't be sidestepped any longer.

Last but not least, she had to be very firm about Dominic staying out of both their lives. She couldn't afford to start being dependent on him for anything. It was going to be hard enough to leave this place when the time came. It would be a thousand times harder if she didn't remain self-sufficient.

It was a few minutes past four when the intercom buzzed again. She raced out to the lobby, then answered the call in as steady a voice as possible.

"We're on our way up," Dominic announced.

Carrie's heart fluttered between excitement and apprehension. But the most important thing was that Dominic had Danny. He had done what he'd said he would do. He had brought her son home to her. And whatever the cost for her to pay in that, Carrie wasn't counting it at this particular moment. It was almost two months since Danny had been taken away from her, and just the thought of seeing him again was pure bliss.

She positioned herself in the centre of the lobby, directly in front of where the elevator doors opened. She was trembling from the sheer force of her emotion when the doors finally slid apart. For a moment, Danny looked stunned, as though he hadn't expected to see her. Then he hurled himself forward, and Carrie dropped to her knees to wrap him in her arms and hug him tight.

"Mum, Mum," he cried in relief and longing and love, almost strangling her as he wound his arms tightly around her neck.

"Oh, Danny! I've missed you so," Carrie half-sobbed, rubbing her cheek against his soft dark hair in her own silent ecstasy of love for this precious child of hers. She was vaguely aware of Dominic Savage stepping out of the elevator, then moving aside, stepping towards the living area, leaving her and Danny alone together. But the focus of her attention was entirely on the little boy who meant so much to her.

"I told them I could look after you, Mum," Danny said fiercely. "But they wouldn't listen. They said you were too sick. And I was so scared you would die and I'd never see you again."

"I know, I know," she soothed. "They said I was too sick to take care of you, Danny. But I'm all right. Truly I am. I'm getting better all the time."

He eased away from her enough to take a good look at her, his blue eyes moist and heartbreaking in their concern for her. "You feel awful thin, Mum."

"I just couldn't eat much, Danny," she explained. "But I can now. I'll soon put weight on. You'll see."

He took a deep breath. "I tried to get back to you, Mum. I was at some place near the Hawkesbury River and I asked the other boys how to get to Ashfield. I would have made it, but I was caught getting onto the train." He pulled a disgusted grimace. "After that they kept a good watch on me and I couldn't get away."

She smiled, her heart so full of love it was almost bursting. "It doesn't matter now, Danny. We're back together again."

He took another deep breath, then grinned his cheeky boy grin. "They sure won't get me another time. I'm staying with you."

"You sure are!" she affirmed vehemently and hugged him again, rocking him in a fierce embrace.

"I was scared coming with Mr. Savage and Mrs. Coombe," he confessed. "I figured you would have come with them if everything was all right. I thought it was a trick to take me somewhere else."

She rubbed his back comfortingly. "I'm sorry, Danny. I wasn't much good at convincing the welfare people that they should give you back to me. And I wanted you so badly, I would have tried anything."

"That's okay, Mum. I was only worried about you." He pushed back to give her his assurance. "Now that I'm here, I'm going to look after you real good."

"I know you will."

He gave her a happy grin, then his head swivelled around. "Where's Mr. Savage?"

Carrie's heart performed a double loop. She knew there was no escaping this final confrontation, but that didn't make it any easier. "I think he went into the living room."

"I'd better speak to him, Mum," Danny said anxiously. "I didn't believe all those things he said to me, so I wouldn't answer him back. He must think I'm awful."

"I think it would be a good idea to thank him. He's gone to a lot of trouble for us. Even lending us this nice place to live in until I'm strong enough to get a job. So we've got a lot to thank him for."

She stood up and took his hand, drawing strength from the strong little fingers that curled around hers.

Dominic was over by the windows in the living room, apparently studying the view of the harbour, but Carrie was not deceived by his seemingly relaxed pose. The taut set of his shoulders betrayed his inner tension.

"Mr. Savage?" Danny called eagerly.

He turned slowly, his eyes sweeping hers with probing intensity before dropping to her boy. She knew it was only natural that he should wonder. She had known that from the moment it became inevitable he would meet Danny. Not that the boy looked like him. He didn't. Unless you counted the blue eyes. But lots of people had blue eyes. It was Danny's age that fed Dominic's speculation.

He made a visible effort to soften his expression. "Happy now?" he asked.

"Yes," Danny replied with feeling. "Thanks a lot, Mr. Savage. I'm sorry for not answering you before. I thought you were tricking me, and until I saw my mum..."

"That's okay, Danny," he said quietly. "But I do need some answers from you now. To enrol you at a school I have to know your age, for a start."

It was done so smoothly, without the slightest hint that anything was amiss. Carrie let the matter of enrolling Danny at school pass for the moment, aware that it was best for everything to be out in the open now.

"I'm seven," came the prompt reply.

Dominic nodded as though it was precisely what he had expected. He posed the critical question without missing a beat. "And when is your birthday, Danny?"

"The tenth of September."

Carrie could see him doing the calculation—a bare eight months from the time they first met. And she could see the disappointment in his eyes. He could not be the father. And then, of course, there were other conclusions he could come to, as well.

Carrie didn't want Dominic's mind dwelling on the sensitive subject of who Danny's father was. Nor did she want any discussion of that painful time in her past. She had taken full responsibility for Danny from the beginning, and it was going to remain that way.

"I'll see about enrolling Danny in a school myself, Dominic," she said briskly. "You've already gone out of your way so much on our behalf, and I'm terribly grateful for all you've done, but there's no need for you to be concerned any further. I can handle everything from now on."

There was a weary mockery in the eyes he raised to hers. "Do you have a particular school in mind?"

She flushed. "There was a primary school at Ashfield. I guess there must be one around here somewhere."

He shook his head. "Some aren't as good as others. I've had practical experience with it. And you're not exactly well, Carrie. Don't you think, for Danny's sake, it's wiser to leave it with me?"

She frowned, feeling that she was being painted into a corner where she didn't want to be, yet she couldn't deny the sense of Dominic's argument. All the same, she wasn't that sick. She could get around the problem if she took it easily.

She lifted pained eyes. "I can cope, Dominic. I don't want to put you to any more trouble."

He gave her a little smile, then shifted his gaze to Danny. It was a severe jolt to Carrie's heart when she saw the question still lingering in Dominic's eyes. It was an even worse jolt when it was followed by a hungry look that said more plainly than words that he wanted this boy to be his own. She suddenly remembered the bleak, frozen stillness that had enveloped him when she had first spoken of her baby. Was that one of the problems in his marriage? Was it childless?

"I don't mind," he said quietly. "You trust me to pick a good school for you, don't you, Danny?"

"Sure!" Danny replied confidently, then shot a worried look at Carrie. "It doesn't matter if Mr. Savage picks my school, does it, Mum? I don't want you getting sick again."

Carrie silently fretted over the situation. Perhaps it was best for Dominic to make the most suitable choice for Danny. She did trust him to do that. Nevertheless, his involvement with her and Danny had to stop. If he kept wanting Danny to be his child... It was a terribly dangerous situation.

"It is necessary to get Danny enrolled quickly, Carrie," Dominic said pointedly.

She heaved a deep sigh and faced him with reluctant resignation. "All right."

The blue eyes were steady with purpose, wiped clear of whatever other thoughts were harboured in his mind. "I'll be in touch when I have it organized."

Carrie looked at him with her own determined purpose. "Just ring me, Dominic. There's no need to visit."

For a moment he challenged that statement, then seemed to accept it. "Very well. I'll get on my way now." He smiled at Danny. "Take good care of your mother. Don't let her overdo things."

"I'll look after Mum. And thanks for everything."

"You're welcome."

There was affection and pride in Dominic's eyes when he turned them back to Carrie.

"Goodbye, Dominic," she said firmly.

"I'll be seeing you, Carrie," he returned softly, and as she watched him leave, Carrie knew this wasn't the end. Dominic wasn't going to let it be the end. Not so long as he had any question about Danny's father in his mind. Sooner or later she was going to have to settle that. Somehow.

CHAPTER SEVEN

IN THE JOY of having Danny home and the worrying issue of Dominic's response to him, Carrie had forgotten all about Mrs. Coombe's visiting program. When she rose the next morning, she certainly did not expect to find the dragon in the dining room setting out a jigsaw puzzle on the table, nor Danny on obviously friendly terms with her.

"Look what Mrs. Coombe brought me!" Danny cried with excitement. "And a whole lot of books and games."

"My sons have long outgrown them," the dragon explained, her stern face incredibly relaxing into benevolence. "I thought they might help keep Danny occupied when you're resting."

Carrie took a deep breath. She could hardly deprive Danny of the pleasure that was so clearly written on his face, yet acceptance of this charity went very much against her independent grain. "That's very kind of you, Mrs. Coombe. And very thoughtful," she forced out as graciously as she could. What else could she say?

"Not at all. I know what boys are like. I've had three of my own. All grown up now and leading their own lives." She heaved a rueful sigh. It made her disconcertingly human. And when she followed it up with an indulgent smile, there was no trace of the sergeant-major at all. "Is there anything you need, dear? I can get it for you before I go to the office."

"Thank you, but we're fine, Mrs. Coombe. Truly," Carrie assured her emphatically. "We won't need anything for a week at least, and then I'm sure I'll be strong enough to do my own shopping, so you mustn't worry about me any more."

The sergeant-major was instantly evoked. Mrs. Coombe rose from her chair in iron command. "You can't be too careful in cases like this. Relapse can be just around the corner. I know. I've given Danny my telephone number. In case he's worried about you over the weekend." She shot Danny some severely lowered eyebrows. "You won't lose it now, will you?"

"No way, Mrs. Coombe! I'm going to look after Mum real good," he promised her. Carrie thought he should have saluted, but instead he only offered a big grin. "And thanks for everything!"

"My pleasure." The sergeant-major beamed approval at him, and Carrie caught some of the afterglow. "You have a fine boy."

"Yes," Carrie meekly agreed, beginning to feel that her independence was being systematically undermined.

Mrs. Coombe definitely departed the victor from this encounter. Having drafted Danny as an enthusiastic and well-rewarded ally, and established herself as an authority on Carrie's state of health, she had effectively squashed all possible protests. Not only that, she had already given Danny his breakfast and Carrie's was waiting for her in the kitchen. It was perfectly plain that when the dragon adopted a stance, it was going to take an awful lot of firepower to shift her.

The kind of firepower Dominic had, Carrie thought. Except she had more than a crawling suspicion that to shift Mrs. Coombe, she had first to shift Dominic. Or perhaps it was the other way around.

Gina arrived. And so did the furniture for Danny's bedroom. All day long! First came a number of segments of a wall unit, which, when all fitted together, formed a chest of drawers, a corner desk, a large set of bookshelves, a corkboard to pin papers on and another desk for a personal computer. It was all made of polished pine and looked first class.

"I decided this room could double as a private study," Gina informed them.

A comfortable and adjustable office chair arrived, upholstered in the same vivid orange as Danny's blanket. A marvellous painting of parrots among tropical foliage was hung on the wall. Another portable television was delivered and installed on the chest of drawers next to Danny's bed. A video recorder came with it. Finally, a massive orange beanbag chair made its appearance.

"The curtains and bedspreads and the decorative cushions for the bed will be a few days," Gina said regretfully, "but it's shaping up very well, don't you think?"

"It's fantastic!" was all Carrie could say.

Danny was in seventh heaven.

"We'll decide what to do with your bedroom on Monday, Carrie," Gina said, glowing with satisfaction. "So start thinking about what you'd fancy having around you. It's so helpful to have your ideas."

Gina had left and Danny was busy putting things away in his new chest of drawers when Dominic telephoned. As soon as Carrie heard his voice, her whole body tensed, fighting against the emotional weakness that threatened her peace of mind.

"How are you today, Carrie?" he asked softly.

"I'm fine," she replied, a little too curtly in reaction to the sudden galloping thump of her heart. She did her best to temper her tone. "Danny and I are both fine, thank you, Dominic."

"I've enrolled Danny in a fine school at Bellevue Hill. He'll be starting on Monday week. There's a good bus service to the school from Circular Quay, so there's no problem with transport. I'll take him myself on the first day and introduce him to the headmaster."

"I can do that, Dominic." She had to stop him from involving himself further with them. It had gone too far already. Just the sound of his voice was disturbing, making her want what she couldn't have.

"I'd like you to be there, Carrie."

The warm eagerness in his tone clouded the sense of what he was saying for a moment. Then Carrie realised he was suggesting that she accompany him, the two of them together, like parents.

"Strangely enough," he continued, "in an imperfect world, these things do matter."

"I meant that *you* don't need to go, Dominic," she said, squirming with embarrassment at the kind of false position that might be presented and feeling more and more desperate to evade any further encounter with him. "I can do it by myself," she added insistently.

Silence for several seconds. Then rather slowly, as though feeling his way with infinite care, he said, "Carrie, I thought... I hope you don't mind. This is for such a relatively short time... It seemed a good idea for Danny to have the best, at least this once. I know the headmaster of this school personally. In fact, he's a former teacher of mine. It would be a discourtesy if I didn't turn up with you."

It was clear that Dominic had used his personal influence to get Danny placed at a really good school. Apparently education rules and regulations could be bent like those at the welfare department for a man of consequence such as Dominic Savage.

"As I said, it's an imperfect world," he acknowledged, perhaps sensing her resentment of how easily this world worked for the big people. "First impressions make a difference, Carrie. I can help," Dominic added persuasively.

That was a reality Carrie couldn't brush aside. It was all too true that little people were ignored or given very little consideration. She had already had a heap of that frustrating experience, and the memory of it was still bitter.

Why should Danny suffer in any way just because she wasn't important like Dominic? Danny was just as good as any other boy and a lot better than most, in her opinion. If Dominic's presence could ensure Danny every advantage the system had to offer, and give him a good start at his new school, then she owed it to her son to accept this one last favour.

"All right, Dominic. Just this once," she conceded, telling herself it would be the very last favour she would accept from him.

"I'll call at the apartment for you. Eight o'clock, Monday week."

He rang off before she could discuss the matter any further. Carrie hadn't even thanked him for making the school arrangements. However, she resisted the impulse to call him back. There were nine days before Danny had to go to school, nine days for her to get a lot stronger. When she saw Dominic on Monday week, she had to make sure she didn't give in to him again, no matter what issue he raised. She had to insist upon complete independence. As it was, she had already accepted too much from him. Although what would she have done without him?

Carrie shook her head. Now she had to learn to live without him all over again. But even that was worth it, just to have Danny back with her.

They had a wonderful weekend. On Saturday they had a leisurely walk through the Botanical Gardens. On Sunday they took a ferry ride up the harbour to Manly and back. They ate well, played some of the games Mrs. Coombe had brought, completed the jig-saw, watched television and generally enjoyed being with each other.

Mrs. Coombe turned up on Monday morning, saying that Mr. Savage had given her the day off to take Danny shopping for his school uniform.

"There's no need!" Carrie protested.

The dragon laid down the law. "You are to rest. Shopping is far too exhausting for you at this stage. Particularly for school clothes, which aren't a simple matter at all. There's sports clothes, proper black shoes, gym shoes, different socks and goodness knows what! It's a long and tedious business and not suitable for a convalescent."

"And Gina wants you here to do your bedroom, Mum," Danny piped up, filling the role of trusty ally to the hilt.

Carrie frowned. Gina had asked for her help. "Then we can go shopping tomorrow, Danny," she insisted.

His face fell. "Why can't I go with Mrs. Coombe?" he demanded.

Which was a difficult question to answer.

"My dear, you must learn to trust me," the dragon said, eyeing Carrie severely.

"Oh, I do, Mrs. Coombe. . . ."

"Then that's settled! Come, Danny!"

Damn, thought Carrie! I've been trapped.

The dragon bore Danny off, an all too eager and willing victim, before Carrie could figure a reasonable way out of the trap. The elevator doors closed on two triumphant smiles. Totally outmanoeuvred, Carrie thought in disgust. The games and books now made perfect sense. Bribery and corruption to win Danny over to her side! But the dragon wasn't going to get away with it a second time, Carrie vowed.

She brooded over Danny's cheerfulness about going off with Mrs. Coombe until Gina arrived and distracted her from that unprofitable train of thought.

"What do you think about apricot as a main theme?" she asked. "Perhaps a floral with that colour so we can highlight it for impact interest."

Carrie was immediately attracted to the idea, and once again they pored over fabric samples. By the time Mrs. Coombe delivered Danny home, along with a formidable array of packages, all the furnishings for the main bedroom had been decided upon.

"Remember what I said about polishing those black shoes every morning, Danny," Mrs. Coombe commanded as she took her leave. "Don't be expecting your mother to do it."

"No, Mrs. Coombe. I mean, yes, I'll remember, Mrs. Coombe," said Danny—the ideal army recruit!

"What about the cost of everything?" Carrie called after her.

"Oh, you'll have to see Mr. Savage about that, dear," the sergeant-major said, passing the buck to a higher authority with sublime confidence in her own position. "I put it all on his credit card."

That night Carrie toted up all the price tags on Danny's new clothes. A good school, she found, cost a lot of money even before the first lesson began. The amount she finally arrived at for the whole school uniform was positively formidable. All of this... for just a short period of time!

Part of the problem was that Mrs. Coombe had bought the best of everything, whereas Carrie would have hunted for bargains. But she supposed she couldn't very well complain. After all, she wasn't paying any rent. Besides, pride whispered, she didn't want Danny to feel he was less well-dressed than the other boys. Although it would make a substantial hole in her wages for some time to come, the clothes wouldn't go to waste. Apart from which, the cost of living was virtually negligible at the present moment.

Thanks to Dominic.

Carrie felt uneasy with this thought. She felt uncomfortably like a kept woman, even though she knew that wasn't the case. She worried over how she could repay Dominic for all he had done for her, but found no satisfactory solution to the problem.

She couldn't ask him to dinner without his wife. The impropriety of such an invitation was all too clear to Carrie, and she instinctively shrank from inviting any meeting with Alyson Hawthorn. She could just imagine how odiously patronising Dominic's bitchy wife would be to her. Carrie knew the attraction had to be there for a marriage to keep going, but she would never understand it. How Dominic could have married that woman...

But he had married her! And that was that! It was none of her business, and she wasn't going to start making it her business. On this last meeting with Dominic at the school for Danny, she had to clear up all outstanding matters so that there would be no need for any further involvement.

The days flew by. Danny's bedroom was completed and looked absolutely marvellous. Carrie's bedroom began to take on a new look with additional pieces of furniture. Fabrics for the furnishings in the living areas were chosen. Gina came and went, milking Carrie for advice on ideas all the time, then delivering the most amazing and wonderful results.

Danny made a point of wearing his new shoes for longer and longer periods each day. Carrie suspected this was on Mrs. Coombe's instructions, but since it *was* sensible, she couldn't very well countermand the sergeant-major's orders. Mrs. Coombe did not reappear until Friday morning, when she came to check that all was how it should be and was told very firmly by Carrie that there was no shopping to be done.

Just for once, the dragon didn't argue or even try to override or outmanoeuvre Carrie. She actually said Carrie looked a lot better, but then spoilt it all by complimenting Danny on looking after his mother so well. It took the shine off Carrie's sense of triumph.

All the same, Carrie was satisfied that she did look better. Her cheekbones were definitely less prominent and her eyes were brighter. However, the state of her hair left a lot to be desired. She eyed Gina's shining cap of auburn hair with envy.

"Who does your hair, Gina?" she asked. "I desperately need something done to mine." It was probably stupid pride, but she felt compelled to look as good as she could when she took Danny to meet the headmaster of his new school. And, of course, it would also be her last meeting with Dominic.

"I'll make an appointment for you with my hairdresser, if you like," Gina instantly offered. "He's a whiz at cutting. Uses a great conditioner, too. I promise you'll look like a million dollars when he finishes with you," she added with an encouraging grin.

Carrie decided this was one time when she wouldn't count the cost. The appointment was made for the next morning, and Gina insisted on taking her and bringing her home, saying it was small enough return for the free lunches Carrie had given her. Danny went with them and was intrigued by all the activity in a hairdressing salon.

"Gosh, Mum! You sure look different now," he remarked when she finally emerged.

She laughed, delighted with the effect of a cleverly shaped bob that curved down to her jawline, and soft feathery bangs, which made her face look softer as well as highlighting her green eyes. Her hair was shining after a long massage with some special conditioner, and Carrie was almost ready to declare Gina's hairdresser a magician.

"Good different, or bad different?" she asked.

"Oh, good!" Danny assured her. "Real pretty like you used to be before you got sick."

Which was certainly telling her straight, Carrie thought ruefully. However she was secretly pleased that Dominic would be left with a nicer memory of the girl he had once known than the image she had re-

cently presented. Not that it was of any real consequence, she told herself. It was sheer vanity on her part
to be thinking like that, and pointless vanity, as well.
In fact, it was flirting with danger to remind Dominic
of those days in any way whatsoever.

On the other hand, it wasn't really for Dominic. Her
improved appearance would certainly make a better
impression at Danny's school, and she wanted Danny
to be proud of his mother. That thought settled any
uneasy twinge of conscience.

Over the weekend, Carrie coached Danny at walking from the apartment to the bus depot at Circular
Quay and back again, making sure he was familiar
with the whole area so that he couldn't possibly get
lost once he started school.

She felt as though her nerves were jumping out of
her skin as she got herself and Danny ready on Monday morning. She rigorously denied to herself that it
was caused by any excitement about seeing Dominic
again. It was simply that starting at a new school was
a big step for Danny. She wanted everything to go
right for him. It was for this reason alone that she
fussed over her appearance.

She wished she had bought a new dress, then chided
herself for craving a needless extravagance. But she
couldn't wear the green shirtmaker. It would remind
Dominic of her fainting fit. Besides, she wanted to
prove to him that she was quite well enough to stand
on her own two feet.

The only other outfit she had with long sleeves was
a lightweight suit in brown and white spotted linen.
She had to make two tucks at the back of the skirt with
safety pins to secure it around her waist, but the hip-
length jacket covered that little adjustment. In fact,

the jacket successfully hid the looseness of her white blouse, as well. She pushed the excess fabric around to the back so she presented a neat smoothness at the front. With some carefully applied apricot lipstick and her blond hair looking bouncy and healthy, Carrie was reasonably satisfied with the result.

Danny looked very smart and suddenly quite heart-wrenchingly grown up in his school uniform. She could hardly call him her baby any more, Carrie acknowledged ruefully. And Mrs. Coombe would have soundly approved the high polish on his new black shoes. You could definitely see your face in them.

They were ready and waiting when Dominic arrived. He stepped out of the elevator and into the apartment on the dot of eight o'clock and took Carrie's breath away with his smile. He looked so impressive in his dark grey business suit, both handsome and commanding, and the blue eyes were as warm and as brilliant as a summer sky.

"Carrie..."

Surprise, pleasure and something deeper and infinitely disturbing rolled through the soft caress of her name. Her heart turned over. The memory of their very first meeting eight years ago leapt into her mind and lingered. He had looked at her just like this...surprised, pleased, wanting to know more of her, wanting...

He wants me now!

And the hell of it is, I still want him!

"That hairstyle really suits you. Although I used to—"

Love it long, Carrie finished for him, remembering how he had stroked it and wound it round his fingers, saying it was like spun silk.

He made a visible effort to check himself, pull back, adopt a less revealing expression. "I do believe you've put on some weight," he said, his gaze roving over her in a far too intimate appraisal.

A flush swept over her skin wherever his gaze alighted, and there was nothing she could do about the erratic acceleration of her heartbeat. "I told you I could get better on my own," she said defensively.

A shadow dimmed the brilliance of his eyes, and he turned quickly to Danny, who was raring to go. "Looks like you've done a good job of looking after your mother, Danny," he said warmly.

"Mum doesn't get tired so fast now," Danny informed him, glowing with pleasure in Dominic's approval. "And we've been eating a real lot."

Dominic laughed and his hand reached out to stroke Danny's hair. Carrie was thrown into more emotional turmoil at the fondly paternal gesture. It was bad enough that Dominic stirred this dreadful yearning in her. Surely he wasn't still harbouring thoughts that Danny might be his. It would be totally unreasonable.

Frantic to get this meeting on a businesslike level, Carrie quickly held out the envelope that contained the cheque she had got from the bank.

"This isn't all I owe you, Dominic, but I'll pay you back the rest when I can," she explained with considerable embarrassment.

He frowned. "As far as I'm concerned, there's no debt between us, Carrie."

The caring in his eyes was almost her undoing. Once again she was drawn back to the time when she had believed that look of caring, believed it so utterly that she thought nothing could have shaken it. But she had read much more into it than there ever was. Besides, she couldn't risk following that treacherous path again. There was not only herself to consider this time. She forced away temptation and gathered her resolution.

"I can't let you pay for Danny's uniform, nor the food Mrs. Coombe bought for us that first morning," she insisted. "Please take it."

The blue eyes warred with the fierce independence in hers, then slowly retreated into a self-mocking resignation. He reached for the envelope and took it without any argument, much to Carrie's relief.

"I guess we'd better be leaving," he said with a rueful little smile. "Ready to go, Danny?"

"I've been ready for ages!" Danny replied with impatient excitement.

As they rode down in the elevator Danny peppered Dominic with questions about the school. Dominic's answers were all reassuring and delivered in a kind indulgent tone, which aroused a deep sadness in Carrie. It suddenly seemed terribly wrong that Danny had always been deprived of a father to stand by his side and do the kind of thing that Dominic was doing for him now. Yet there was nothing she could do about it. And even if she could live the past over again, she would not have chosen differently. There had never been any other way.

A wave of deep depression rolled over her as they settled into the luxurious comfort of the Daimler. She told herself she should be grateful that Dominic had accepted her independent stance, that there was no longer any reason for them to see each other again, and that there could be no more crossin҃
their lives. This car alone hammered h҃

ferent stations in life. It was part and parcel of the kind of marriage he had.

But she didn't feel grateful. She felt wretchedly miserable. And not even her love for Danny could fill that other aching emptiness in her life.

It was almost agony sitting beside Dominic, being aware of everything about him, remembering how it had once been between them, listening to him chat so charmingly with Danny and Danny's eager response to his interest. She wished she could touch him, look openly at him, meet his eyes with that special intimate togetherness she had once shared with him.

If only they could be taking Danny to school like real parents who were proud of their son. But she couldn't afford to indulge in that fantasy. It could never never happen. She had to accept that. And the intimate togetherness she thought she had once shared with Dominic was only an illusion. She had to keep remembering that, as well.

If she slipped up, if she let Dominic see how she felt about him, she suspected he would have no more conscience about taking what he wanted than he had in the past. If an engagement had not been any impediment to gratifying his desire for her, a marriage was not going to get in his way, either. Particularly the kind of open marriage he undoubtedly had with Alyson. However much she wanted him, Carrie would not accept being a fling on the side. The consequences of that were all too clear to ⊦

The Daimler slowed⟋ Carrie was too deep in thought to take⟋ had been halted by traffic scores ⟋ o Bellevue Hill.
⟋ t expectation in

It startled her into looking out the window, and Carrie instantly suffered another shock. Superb and immaculately kept playing fields seemed to stretch forever. Everything about the school—tennis courts, swimming pool, gardens, the grounds, the buildings themselves—trumpeted wealth. Old wealth! This was no ordinary public school. It had to be one of the most elite private schools in Sydney!

"This is it," Dominic confirmed, turning the car through a wrought-iron gateway.

Carrie barely had time to recover from her shock before they were parked in a special visitors' bay in front of what was obviously the administrative building. Then Danny was scrambling out of the car, almost jumping out of his skin in excitement, and Dominic made a swift exit as well, striding around to open Carrie's door for her. Her eyes stabbed a thousand tortured questions at him as he helped her out. He fended them off with a look of brick-wall determination.

I'm trapped again, Carrie thought despairingly, as Danny joined them, chattering nineteen to the dozen, obviously thrilled that this marvellously impressive place was *his* school. The arrangements had been made, his clothes had been bought, and they were here, on the brink of meeting the headmaster.

Somehow Carrie could not force out the words to declare the whole proceedings null and void. It was wrong. It was all terribly wrong. And there was a dreadful panic welling up inside her at the thought of what this might all mean. But when Dominic took her arm and steered her towards the path that led to the arched entrance ahead of them, she could not find the strength of resolution to make a sensible stand. With Danny looking on, listening, it just wasn't possible!

Once inside, they were immediately ushered to the headmaster's office. Dominic's old teacher welcomed them warmly and was most interested in the fact that Danny had spent most of his life in Fiji. Danny was asked a lot of questions, which he answered with an uninhibited confidence, stirring Carrie's maternal pride, despite all her underlying misgivings about the whole situation.

"I think young Danny might turn out to be as good a scholar as you were, Dominic," the headmaster declared, obviously pleased with the interview. "You can leave him with me now. I'll take him to meet his teachers personally."

This was certainly favoured treatment, and Carrie felt profoundly embarrassed as she recognised the speculation in the headmaster's eyes throughout their leave-taking. He was undoubtedly putting one and one together and getting more than two. Although nothing overt was said either by Dominic or the headmaster, Carrie sensed that some private understanding had been reached between them when the arrangements had been made.

Carrie hoped that she had performed creditably enough, for Danny's sake, but she was churning inside as Dominic escorted her to the Daimler. As soon as they were both enclosed within the intimate privacy of the car, she turned on him with all the vehemence of feeling that the meeting had aroused.

"You had no right to enrol Danny in this school, Dominic," she said to him.

His mouth set grimly as he switched on the engine, put the car into gear and drove it towards the gate.

"Why not?" he finally replied, a fine tension edging the calm, reasonable tone he employed.

"You know why not," she accused. "The fees must be astronomical. And you didn't consult me."

"You wanted a good school for Danny. You agreed to leave the choice to me. I know this is a good school."

"That's not the point!"

"I took responsibility for the fees. And they weren't so high, Carrie. It's the school I attended throughout my primary education, and old boys have certain privileges. Discounts..."

"I'm not stupid, Dominic!" Carrie retorted angrily. "That kind of thing only ever relates to families."

His face tightened, but he spoke very quietly and with slow, deliberate emphasis. "How do I know that Danny isn't part of me, Carrie?"

Her heart stopped dead, then catapulted into mad overtime. It was finally out in the open! And she had to answer it! But how?

"I'd like to reach a better understanding with you, Carrie," Dominic said softly. "And I'd rather try to do that when I'm not driving in peak-hour traffic. Would you mind if I come up to your apartment when we get back?"

There was a dreadful tightness in her throat. Her voice sounded half-strangled as she replied, "I think...I think that's a good idea."

Carrie was not sure it was a good idea at all, but Dominic's actions in regard to Danny left her little choice. She should have resolved the matter before, when she had seen the questions in his eyes. She had taken the coward's way out. Yet to go through all that hurt again, to go back through all that had happened . . . She closed her eyes and willed herself to be strong.

What had to be done, had to be done!

She could not allow herself and Danny to be drawn into Dominic's kind of life, no matter what considerations he offered her! She fiercely wished she had never gone to him, never let him back into her life for any reason. The risk she had taken, for Danny's sake, had been too high. It was now paramount to convince Dominic that he had no reason to pursue a relationship with either one of them.

CHAPTER EIGHT

THE JOURNEY TO CIRCULAR Quay was accomplished in far too fast a time for Carrie. Nevertheless, she did determine one thing. Some questions she would not answer. Those she did, however, would be entirely truthful. In that regard, she would not deceive Dominic.

He kept a grim silence, even on the elevator ride to the apartment. Carrie's stomach was in knots when she finally led the way into the living room. It was still empty apart from the blue-grey leather armchairs and the coffee table. Today was one of the days Gina was out scouting for the right furniture for it, so they were completely alone. There was no risk of interruption.

"Do you want to sit down?" she asked with stiff politeness, making an awkward gesture towards the armchairs.

"You sit, Carrie," he returned quietly.

But she knew she couldn't relax, couldn't even appear to relax. She dropped her handbag on one of the chairs and moved on, stepping over to the windows, pretending to take in the harbour view because she didn't want to meet Dominic's eyes.

"I applied for a copy of Danny's birth certificate."

It felt like an iron fist was squeezing her heart. "You had no right to do that, Dominic. It's an invasion of privacy."

"I thought I might have a right, Carrie," he suggested softly. "The father's name is not filled in."

"It usually isn't in the case of an illegitimate birth."

She heard the hard edge to her voice and winced. But she had to be hard. This was no time to be weak. She waited patiently, all her senses as alert as they had ever been in her whole life. This was the moment of truth. What she had gone out of her way to avoid all these years.

"Danny was born eight months after—" he was going to say our affair, but he changed to "—eight months after we were together."

Carrie kept her face impassive. This is how people play poker, she told herself. She committed herself to a clipped, "You already know that."

His next words were more tentative, but determinedly probing nevertheless. "Sometimes, even the most well-intended precautions aren't a hundred percent safe. Accidents happen." He paused, waiting for her to comment.

The iron fist squeezed even tighter. She said nothing.

"And some babies are born prematurely," he continued, relentlessly pressing the question.

She waited, waited for the inevitable.

"Carrie, is that what happened to you?"

Somehow she forced the necessary words out. "However hard it is for you to accept, Dominic, most pregnancies go full term."

There was a long nerve-tearing silence. Then slowly, painfully, Dominic dragged out his next question. "Are you telling me that you were already pregnant by some other man at the time we were together?"

Her mind and heart were awash with sheer agony. Carrie knew she had to take the initiative. Otherwise these statements and future questions would never stop. She summoned up all her willpower, commanded her body not to betray her in any way, fixed a mask of calm indifference on her face then slowly swung around.

Dominic was no more than a few paces away, and the pained look on his face triggered a surge of savage resentment. What did he know of pain? He had taken his pleasure, hadn't he? Then moved back to Alyson having enjoyed his little fling on the side.

"Are you criticising my life-style, Dominic?" she demanded harshly.

His head jerked back as though she had hit him, and she could see his inner torment warring on his face, darkening his eyes. I've lost him, she thought, lost him forever. And all her fierce resentment dwindled into the deep inner chasm of emptiness she had carried for so long. But then she remembered she had never had him. This confrontation was not about her. It was about Danny. And she would not let Dominic or anyone else make an emotional battleground over the child she had borne and raised.

She saw acceptance gradually emerge from his torment, but Carrie felt no relief. The emptiness spread through her whole body, making her feel numb, beyond pain or any other feeling or emotion.

"I'll never criticise you, Carrie."

She heard the words, even registered that they were spoken in a gentle, forgiving tone. On a rather distant level her mind kept ticking over. She wondered if he regretted the way he had played musical beds. Probably not, she surmised. However liberated women were today, there were still different standards for men and women. And always would be. Particularly where children were concerned. The more things changed, the more they stayed the same. Because the pain was still there, just as always.

She turned to the window and stared at the water traffic in the harbour, vaguely noting the ever-widening wakes left by the boats as they carved their way through the water. Her time with Dominic had had a long wake, but it was over now. And whatever kind of possessiveness had been aroused in him by the thought of Danny being his child would quickly be laid to rest. She did not want to watch him go. She had to lay her own ghosts to rest. Forever.

Dominic did not go. He came up behind her, his fingers curling lightly over her shoulders. His head was near hers. She could feel his breath on the newly cropped nape of her neck. Her mind told her that he wanted something more from her. Some appeasement, perhaps, for all the trouble he had gone to.

"I'm sorry you're disappointed in me, Dominic," she pushed out huskily. Her throat was dry, like the lonely desert inside her.

"Not disappointed. Other things," he murmured vaguely.

Carrie didn't question what the other things were. She didn't want to know what they were. Things said could never be retracted, and they caused too much hurt. Best left unstated. Just let me go, Dominic, she thought, unable to summon the energy to voice the words. Let it all go.

His mouth grazed over her hair, down by her ear. His lips touched her cheek, a light tender pressure that stirred a tingle of life...of need. Carrie leant back against him, angled her face towards him, then belatedly realised what she was doing. The impulse to turn around in his arms, to accept his kisses until she was totally mindless, to beg him to make love to her, to lead him to her bed...that impulse rampaged through her body with almost irresistible force.

But he was married, the voice of sanity reminded her. He had a wife. Maybe even children. But she didn't want to know about that. And she had to stop this madness before it took hold of her. She turned her head away from the tempting contact.

"I don't think...you should touch me, Dominic. That's not fair." Somehow she couldn't put the proper amount of coldness into her voice. Rather, the words were said with all the aching love and tenderness in her heart.

She felt Dominic's body stiffen against her. Then abruptly he moved away. "I'm sorry," he rasped, and the gravelled anguish of loneliness in the brusque apology smote her brittle defences.

Alyson was no partner for him. Every intuition Carrie had was screaming out that he shared the same bleak emptiness she herself felt. The thought that she could have let Dominic make love to her came unbidden to her mind, and it took a lot of stern repression to make it go away. Such an act was no solution, but the beginning of the end. For her.

"You don't have to be sorry." Inadequate words she knew, and said so stiltedly that Dominic surely had to take them as the ultimate rejection of anything between them, even sympathy.

But still he did not go.

She heard him pacing the floor behind her, apparently struggling to come to terms with the situation.

Carrie remained where she was, staring blindly out the window, unseeing and forcing herself to be uncaring. Or as uncaring as she could be. Eventually he stopped moving. She heard him draw in a deep breath and slowly expel it. When he spoke his voice was quiet and carefully drained of any emotion.

"So you came to me on the rebound. From some other love affair that ended unhappily."

"Something like that," Carrie agreed dully.

"No wonder things worked out the way they did. That explains so much."

His voice sounded as dull and despairing as her own. Carrie remained silent. She had no more to say. If Dominic thought everything was explained, however he had worked it out, there would be no more questions.

He gave a mirthless little laugh. "The great irony," he said savagely, "is that all the precautions we took to stop you getting pregnant were unnecessary and useless."

Carrie felt a well of unjustified anger surging destructively over the control she was trying so hard to keep. "As it turned out," she said curtly, once again turning to face him, her green eyes blazing her condemnation of his unkind mockery, "and with the benefit of hindsight, yes! They were useless! That much is certainly true."

The sudden passion in her voice startled him, shocked him.

"But, Dominic," Carrie plunged on, uncaring what his reaction was, just desperate to get this over, "I do not wish to discuss *our affair*." She enunciated those two words with particular emphasis, needing to get the past stamped with its actual reality. "I certainly do not wish to have it recollected with a blow-by-blow description!"

He winced, his mouth twisting into a pained grimace. Then he shook his head in an anguished denial before finally bringing himself under control and facing her with bleak resignation. "I guess it's time for me to go," he said flatly.

"I think that's the best decision," she affirmed, and regretted how distant—how callous—she must sound. Yet there was nothing that could be retrieved from this situation.

"At least I'm grateful to you for putting our...*relationship*—" he stressed the word with bitter irony "—into its proper perspective. I had the wrong impression. I thought it was different from what it was."

He turned away.

Carrie was too stung by those words to hold her tongue. The impulse of anger and scorn proved too strong. Why was the woman always held to blame? "I don't know what you think," she said in frayed anguish. "It doesn't matter any more now than it did then." Bitterness crept into her voice. "But whatever else you may think of me, at least *I* never played musical beds."

He paused in mid-stride, turned swiftly, violent emotion working over his face. "Are you implying that I did?"

Carrie shrugged indifferently, but her green eyes flicked scorn at the supposed innocence he was projecting. "You are what you are. What you do is none of my business."

She knew she had made a bad mistake even before she saw his expression change. She should have kept her mouth shut and let him go, no matter how unfair a slur he cast on her for the breakup that his attitudes had caused. All she had done with her stupid pride was prolong the inevitable and make it even more tortured.

Dominic stood absolutely still. All conflict had been wiped from his face. He could have been a statue except for his eyes. They probed hers with intense directness, as though trying to bore through to her soul. Carrie met them with all the resistance she could muster, denying him entry to the churning cauldron of emotion this delay had provoked.

His brow furrowed in thought. There was a perceptible straightening of his shoulders. His chin angled with determination, his brow cleared of its furrows, and a look of resolution transformed his face.

"So, everything is resolved," he said enigmatically, "and yet nothing is resolved."

A devil-may-care look glittered into his eyes and curled his mouth into a provocative little smile. He covered the floor space between them with a casual stride that belied the tension Carrie felt sweeping from him and entangling her in his purpose. She didn't move. Somehow she couldn't. Her heart was slamming against her chest as he lifted a hand and gently cupped her cheek. His thumb tilted her chin with a persuasive little caress.

"There is one last thing I have to know, Carrie," Dominic said softly. "And I figure there's only one way I can find out."

He took her by surprise, his head bending swiftly to her own, his lips sealing hers with a seductive sensuality that sent shock waves through her entire body. She trembled, and a strong arm instantly scooped her against the warm security of his body. She felt her mouth softening pliantly to the persuasive movement of his and told herself to pull away, to stop him before... before his tongue started its tantalising temptation... before she succumbed to its erotic invitation to deepen this forbidden intimacy... before she gave in to the need that screamed to let him do as he liked because she liked it, too... wanted it... craved it.

And then it was too late.

He kissed her with all the passion of a starving man, and her eight-year hunger rose to meet his in overwhelming waves, drowning her conscience, drowning any thought of past or future, feasting on all that was offered and could be taken now, no matter what hell had to be paid later. Perhaps it was the despair lurking somewhere in her subconscious that inspired her mad wantonness, that made her wind her arms around Dominic's neck in feverish possessiveness, that made her press her body to his in blind seeking need, that made her ride this wild roller coaster of total insanity, and all because sanity was suddenly too hard to bear.

It was Dominic who withdrew first, lifting his mouth from hers and showering her face and hair with impassioned kisses. "I thought I'd lost you," he breathed in a whisper of yearning that found a deep echo inside Carrie. "Lost you forever." Then in a burst of relief, "But it's not so. Thank God it's not so."

His arms tightened around her. His lips trailed down to her ear. "You can't deny me now, Carrie," he pleaded softly. "Say you love me."

The words were there, imbedded in her heart, quivering for the expression he demanded. Carrie wanted to say them. She had promised herself she would speak

only the truth to Dominic. Had to speak the truth.
And her body had already betrayed that truth, anyway. Yet the memory of what had happened last time
came back to haunt her. It was all too one-sided.
Where was his commitment to her? He asked too
much. And he would leave her to go back to his wife,
his marriage.

She opened her eyes and lifted her head back to
challenge him. "Why don't you say those words to
me, Dominic?"

The blue eyes caressed her with all the promises she
could wish for. "I love you, Carrie. I always did love
you. Only you."

He said the words slowly, simply. Carrie could almost believe they were true. Dominic Savage, the ultimate deceiver, a bitter voice whispered. And he
hadn't changed. The only difference now was that the
impediment to any serious relationship between them
was out in the open. And being conveniently ignored
by him.

"And that's why you married someone else, Dominic?" she asked scornfully.

"What does that matter now?" he pleaded. "Now
that we've found each other again."

A bitter little laugh erupted from her throat. "It
may seem odd to you in this day and age, but it does
matter to me. It matters very deeply."

Anguish darkened his eyes and roughened his voice.
"Carrie, you must know from your own experience
that there are different kinds of relationships. We had
something special between us. And it's still there. For
me and for you, Carrie. I need you in my life. And I
think you need me just as much."

It was a need she had learnt to stifle long ago, and she simply had to keep on stifling it. Her green eyes were hard and implacable as she delivered her reply. "Let's not fantasise, Dominic. You are as much a realist as I am. There's no going back." Not even to assuage his loneliness, or hers, she added silently. However unsatisfactory he was finding his marriage, she was not going to let him use her to make up for it.

He shook his head. "I don't understand you, Carrie. Your lips, your body, are so soft and pliant...telling me what I want to hear from you. Yet your mind is like steel."

Her mouth twisted with sad irony. "Put me down as an aberration in your life."

"And if I won't?"

She dragged her hands down to press lightly against his shoulders. Every jagged nerve in her body clamoured a vehement protest at the thought of breaking from his embrace, of severing the body contact that was still arousing so many pleasurable sensations. She hesitated, riven once more by temptation.

Could she live with being Dominic's woman on the side? Did it really matter that he was cheating on Alyson? After all, with her attitudes, she was undoubtedly cheating on him.

But where could it lead?

And what about the effect on Danny?

No. She couldn't be blindly selfish. Nor did she want to face the consequences of another fling with Dominic. She shook her head.

"There's no future for us, Dominic," she stated flatly.

It was he who released her from his embrace, lifting his hands to cradle her face with infinite tenderness. His eyes begged indulgence from hers. "Carrie, I don't believe you. I can't. And I won't. I don't think you know your own mind. You've been under so much strain lately—"

"It's not that."

A finger instantly slid to her lips in a soft, silencing caress. "Don't say no to me, Carrie. Think about it. Think about how you felt with me just now. Think of how it might be . . . for us . . . together. I'd be good for Danny. As if he were my own son. At least think about trying it, Carrie."

Dear heaven! He knew how to twist the knife!

He removed his finger and dropped a light and infinitely sweet kiss on her lips. "I won't pressure you, Carrie. Perhaps this has all been too much for you too quickly. Just think about it. And let me know."

He touched her mouth again with his fingertips, as though sealing his kiss there as a lingering memory. His eyes made their demand with more compelling intensity.

Then he turned and left her.

To think about it.

And let him know.

CHAPTER NINE

CARRIE DID THINK ABOUT IT—hard—because it was all too easy to let her emotions influence her thoughts. She wanted Dominic Savage. Had always wanted him. There had been no other man in her life since she had left him eight years ago. She *wanted* to believe she had made some dreadful mistake then, that he had really loved her and it wasn't just a fling to him. Even though it meant that all these years had been wasted, Carrie still wanted to believe Dominic had always loved her.

But it wasn't true.

She knew it couldn't be true.

It simply didn't add up that way.

From the very beginning she had felt it was too good to be true. Their meeting had been like a fantasy, and of course, that was precisely what it was.

The two weeks at Surfers' Paradise was to be her first real holiday away from home and away from her mother. She had saved all year for it. On her very first night there she had visited Jupiters Casino. Not to gamble. Just to look, because it seemed to be the most glamorous place to go. She had been intrigued by the people there and the games being played.

Dominic had been at one of the blackjack tables. As soon as Carrie saw him, the rest of the huge gambling hall faded into total insignificance. She watched him play. He looked up and caught her watching him. He had smiled at her, and Carrie had smiled back in automatic response. The compelling blue eyes began inviting her involvement, sending her twinkling signals—should he sit on the cards he had or buy in for another one? The silent flirtation was the most exciting thing that had ever happened to Carrie.

He didn't play for very long. He gave his seat to someone else and literally swept Carrie away, taking her to the disco, to supper, then inviting her home with him to the fabulous apartment on the beachfront. She knew he was out of her class even before then, but she had stars in her eyes and didn't want to see any reason she shouldn't be with Dominic. She might be Cinderella compared to him, but that didn't mean she couldn't enter his world, particularly when he had invited her and wanted her there with him.

They had two idyllic weeks together—every girl's dream. Dominic had pampered her. Cost was no object. He took her everywhere, showed her all the tourist highlights on the Gold Coast. Carrie could have whatever she wanted. Not that she wanted much. Just to be with Dominic. The time she enjoyed most was when he brought out his guitar and sang to her as they sat on the balcony at night, with the stars overhead and the ocean a soft background thrum to the seductive lilt of Dominic's fine tenor voice. When he had asked her to stay on with him for the entire month of her vacation leave, Carrie had been only too happy to do so.

The problem started when Dominic's crowd arrived, and it was immediately obvious that whoever had planned this group holiday had not planned for Carrie. There was one female too many. Her! And they very smartly let Carrie know it in subtle and not so subtle ways.

Carrie hadn't liked Alyson Hawthorn from the first. Alyson, Carrie recognised, was trouble with a capital *T.* Nor had she trusted her. Even when she was all sweetness and light towards Carrie in front of Dominic, the sweetness had a streak of acid and the light invariably had a shade of condescension.

Carrie didn't fit in with the crowd at all, and they were as quick to realise it as she was. They were more Dominic's age than hers, sophisticated in their attitudes, widely travelled and used to all the trappings that money could buy. They teased Carrie unmercifully—at least the women did—although never in front of Dominic.

At first Carrie had played it down. If she had Dominic, it didn't matter. She might be a square peg in a round hole, but she could grin and bear it. They were Dominic's friends, although she found it difficult to believe. They were so different to him. Yet this was the kind of social set to which he belonged.

She would have endured it, and perhaps in time come to learn how to be more sophisticated herself. She never got the opportunity. The climax came within a few days.

Dominic had gone with his friends to surf while the girls sunned on the beach. Carrie had excused herself to do a bit of necessary shopping, but eventually, reluctantly, she returned and forced herself to join the others on the beach.

Alyson instantly started baiting her. "What's it like to be in love, Carrie?"

The other five girls tittered their amusement at what was coming.

"I'm coping very well," Carrie had snapped back.

"Oh, honey! You are such an innocent," Alyson had patronised. "I bet you were a virgin. And Dominic fancied being your tutor. But you can't expect to keep him, you know. It's really only kind to warn you you're simply a temporary aberration, a little fling on the side."

"I don't believe you," Carrie had protested vehemently.

Alyson had shrugged. "More fool you, honey! But if you need some hard evidence to get things into perspective—" she held out her left hand and waggled a huge diamond solitaire ring in front of Carrie's eyes "—this is the ring Dominic gave me as a token of *serious* intentions."

If it had just been Alyson, Carrie wouldn't have believed it. Even when all the other girls agreed that Alyson and Dominic were indeed engaged to be married, she still clung to the belief that it was some cruel, sick joke. But they had an answer for everything.

To the question about Dominic's blatant infidelity, they had mocked her with knowing grins. "We all do it," Alyson explained condescendingly. "But when it comes to marriage, honey, that's really about property. Money marries money. It's the way the world turns."

"Why haven't you been wearing the engagement ring before?" Carrie had demanded hotly.

Alyson's smile was a belittling taunt. "Dominic fancied a bit more time with you."

"So why are you showing it to me now?"

Alyson heaved an impatient sigh. "I'm not the jealous type, but I am getting a bit sick of those gooey green eyes following Dominic around like a dog, and him petting you along. The problem with Dominic is that he's always been too kindhearted. Particularly with underdogs. It's time you woke up. I mean, you really are getting to be a drag on the whole holiday. You're not with it, and you're keeping Dominic out of it.''

The other girls were very vocal in seconding that opinion.

Alyson delivered the final punch with infinite weariness. ''Why not do us all a favour, Carrie, and get the hell out of here? You're so far out of your depth it's not even funny any more. Dominic's done you enough favours these last few weeks. He's given you a good time, hasn't he? So do something for him. Make a quick, easy break of it. Just hop on a bus and go back to wherever it is you belong and play with your own kind.''

So much of what Alyson said struck true, even past Carrie's blind love for Dominic. Too sick at heart to brave out a confrontation with him in front of Alyson, Carrie had gone to the apartment and packed her things. It was impossible for her to stay on, given the attitude of his friends towards her, and even more impossible if all they said was true. But she didn't want to go without speaking to Dominic first. However painful that might be, she still nursed a little hope that he truly shared what she felt for him.

When she had finished packing, she watched from the living room windows, waiting for him to finish surfing. When he finally walked up the beach, Alyson went to meet him. They talked. He gripped her upper arms as though thinking of drawing her into an embrace, then apparently dropped the idea to take the towel she had brought to him. He accompanied her to where the others were grouped together, then lay down on the beach with them.

His life.

His world.

And the woman he would marry.

The despair she had felt then was the same despair she felt now. Nothing had changed as far as she and Dominic were concerned. She was still a fling on the side in his mind, a *different* relationship to that which he maintained with his wife.

The most sensible course was to get right out of his life, as she had eight years ago. Not discuss it with him. Just do it! Except that that wasn't quite so simple in her present circumstances. And she wanted him, even more now than she had then. She wanted him for herself and also for Danny.

Carrie's mind kept going around in torturous circles, but no matter which way her thoughts leaned, there was still one inescapable fact. Dominic was married. He might be able to ignore that fact, but Carrie couldn't. To have a relationship with a married man, even though he was married to *that* woman, was not acceptable.

If Dominic really loved her and wanted her to share his life, to be together, to be a father to Danny, he had to divorce Alyson.

She could let him know that!

But quite obviously that was not what he wanted to hear. Or he would have said it himself!

It came as a shock to her when Danny arrived home from school. She hadn't noticed the time passing. She was still in the suit she had worn this morning and hadn't even thought of having lunch. Danny was ravenous after his exciting day, and Carrie immediately set about supplying them both with a sumptuous afternoon tea. She couldn't afford to let herself get weak again.

Her heart shrank as she listened to Danny extoll the wonders of his new school—Dominic's old school—which was clearly beyond her means and status in life. Danny liked all his teachers. The sporting facilities were super, and there was even a computer room where the mysteries of computers were turned into easy-to-learn skills.

"And the teacher said we have a lesson on how to use them every Tuesday afternoon and Friday afternoon. I can't wait till tomorrow!" he enthused. "We never had computers in Fiji."

As she listened to his excited comments about this new kind of education, Carrie found some consolation in the thought that she had been right in her decision to leave Fiji. She wanted Danny to have every opportunity to pursue whatever ambitions he might nurse as time went by. Fiji was a fine place to live, but it provided only limited opportunities for the young.

Times had changed so much since she had been at school, Carrie reflected. The whole world was changing with the escalation of new technology. She wondered if the public schools were as well equipped with computers as the wealthy private school Dominic had chosen for Danny. Probably not, she decided.

If she agreed to what Dominic wanted, Danny could stay at that school and probably have the best education money could buy. Maybe that was worth bending her morals. Maybe Dominic would be good for Danny in lots of ways. He could give him so much that Carrie couldn't, and never would be able to by herself.

And Danny liked him. Of course, that was only natural since Dominic had rescued him from the welfare institution and brought him back to her. And all the exciting things that had been happening since Dominic had entered their lives—this fabulous apartment, the new clothes, the school. It had to affect Danny's opinion of Dominic.

And all the good things would go on, if she agreed to what Dominic wanted.

But for how long?

And eventually Danny would start asking questions about their relationship. How would she answer those questions?

Carrie repressed her inner turmoil as much as she could and concentrated hard on responding naturally to Danny's excitement. But it was a relief when his bedtime finally came.

She lay awake for a long time that night, a host of wayward desires fighting hard common sense, which dictated that she had to cut her association with Dominic as soon as she could. The longer it went on, the harder the break would become, both for her and Danny. It would be easier for Danny to adjust to a new school if he wasn't given the time to settle too comfortably into this one.

The next day she started on job applications. Every morning she checked the listings for positions vacant in the *Sydney Morning Herald.* There weren't many, not in the locations she preferred, but whenever she found the odd one or two, she wrote to them.

The days slipped from one week into the next. Carrie kept on writing about jobs and waited anxiously for some response to come by mail. She wished people could make up their minds as fast as she had to. Although Dominic had said he would wait for a response from her without pressure, she suspected he would not wait indefinitely. Yet she shied away from contacting him in any way whatsoever, afraid she might weaken without the bolster of a decisive commitment to a job somewhere.

The furnishing of the apartment continued at a high rate of knots. Gina was totally indefatigable in determining what should be done and doing it. Carrie grew concerned that everything would be finished and she still wouldn't have anywhere definite to go. It was some secret relief to her when Gina declared there would be quite a long wait—two months at least—for the dining room furniture, which was being made to order. Surely by then, Carrie kept assuring herself, she would have succeeded in securing a job and knowing where she had to move for it.

The decorating served to fill Carrie's days with much-needed distraction while Danny was at school, and Gina was always stimulating and cheerful company. Carrie learnt quite a lot about the art of interior decorating, and Gina picked up a number of helpful hints about the preparation and presentation of various meals. It was a mutually satisfying and rewarding association.

Then, several weeks since she had last seen Dominic, Dr. Burridge called at the apartment. Carrie instantly realised that Dominic had sent him to check up on her. She felt a twinge of guilt. After all Dominic had done for her—for whatever reasons—she should have at least telephoned him to allay any further concern over her state of health. While she had no desire whatsoever to submit to another medical examination, Carrie felt it would be ungrateful and discourteous to turn the doctor away.

Besides which, she didn't have to take any notice of what Dr. Burridge said. She knew she was getting better almost every day now. Only occasionally did she get a slight attack of dizziness, and that was invariably when she had bent over for something and straightened up too fast. She could walk quite long distances without feeling exhausted, and her clothes were definitely not just hanging on her any more.

Indeed, when she admitted the doctor to the apartment, his surprise at her improved appearance told its own tale. Nevertheless, he still wanted to use the dreaded stethoscope on her, and Carrie resigned herself to the vagaries of medical science once again.

"Well, young lady, I have to concede you didn't need further hospitalisation after all," he finally declared with a satisfied smile. "You've managed very well all by yourself. In fact, one of my best cases."

Carrie couldn't resist a triumphant little snipe. "So, I did the right thing. I got better all by myself."

"I'll put it this way," the doctor pontificated. "This time it worked out all right." Then more thoughtfully, "Of course, if I hadn't thought it would work out for you, I'd have been back much sooner. With you, I had to use one of the most advanced techniques known to the medical profession."

Carrie looked at him dumbfounded. "You believe you had something to do with me getting better?"

"Of course."

Carrie felt a surge of righteous indignation. She just couldn't let him get away with such an outrageous statement. "What technique did you use?" she demanded.

"Masterly inactivity. Only the very finest doctors have the judgement to use it."

"In other words, let nature take its course," Carrie interpreted very drily, wondering if Dr. Burridge thought he had invented nature, and if God would one day tick him off for such arrogance.

"It's a sad truth that many hospital beds are filled with patients suffering iatrogenic diseases," he proclaimed, continuing his medical jargon. "A wise doctor knows when to leave well enough alone."

Carrie decided the wise doctor needed pinning down again. "What does iatrogenic mean?"

Dr. Burridge gave a delicate little cough. "Uh, a physician induced condition."

"Doctors' guinea pigs," Carrie retorted with forthright indelicacy. "I thought as much."

"As I said before, it's often best to let nature take its course."

"So you're not advising me to do anything other than what I am doing."

A sly twinkle entered the doctor's eyes. "There's only one other thing you can do that will bring about a more rapid recovery."

"What's that?" Carrie asked sceptically.

"Fall in love, my dear. That's the greatest healer. Definitely the greatest healer. Fall in love. I can give you no greater advice."

Carrie regarded him with grave suspicion. Was he playing Dominic's hand for him, or had the doctor himself perceived too much from that first meeting in Dominic's office? "That, I'm afraid, is far too extreme," she said drily.

"Not at all," the doctor disagreed with a confident smile. "Love is extremely useful and beneficial."

Carrie didn't argue. The man obviously meant well.
She could have told him that two beneficial weeks of
falling in love was not useful at all when it was totally
crushed by the overwhelming weight of an eight-year
aftermath of emotional wear and tear. However, Carrie didn't voice any of these concerns. She gave Dr.
Burridge the benefit of a confident and dazzling-with-
health smile as she saw him out, so that he would
never have any reason to come back.

With her conscience eased by the thought that the
doctor's report would cover any legitimate concern
Dominic had for her, Carrie continued her dogged efforts to find a new situation for herself and Danny.

She had finished writing another application two
days later, and was feeling somewhat let down that all
her efforts so far had been of little avail. She began
idly flipping through the rest of the newspaper, even
to the social pages, which she rarely read. A photograph caught her eye. She did not have to read the
caption to know who it was. Alyson Hawthorn. Alyson Savage, Carrie corrected herself.

Her first impulse was to quickly turn the page and
shut the woman out of her mind. To look at Alyson
only reminded her of Dominic. And that hurt too
much. She thrust the newspaper away from her and
determinedly ignored it by going out to post the application.

But somehow, when she returned to the apartment,
a dreadful fascination drew her to the photograph.
Carrie told herself it was morbid curiosity about the
kind of life that Dominic's wife led. However stupidly masochistic it was of her to want to know anything about it, she couldn't help herself. She had to

look, to read, to prove she was doing the right thing by denying Dominic the relationship he wanted with her.

Alyson was not alone in the photograph. She was with a man who looked old enough to be her father. And probably was, Carrie thought, until she read the caption that accompanied the photograph. "Smiles from proud parents-to-be, socialite Alyson Hawthorn and brewery magnate Howard Slater, who confirm they will be married as soon as their separate divorces have been finalised."

Carrie's eyes read and reread the words, hardly daring to believe them. Alyson had reverted to her maiden name. And she was pregnant. But not by Dominic.

Her heart ricocheted around her chest as the meaning of the caption finally sank into her mind and gave birth to a wild leap of hope and joy.

Dominic's marriage to Alyson was over!

He was free!

As good as free!

There was no impediment to pursuing a relationship with him, a lifelong relationship! And Dominic wasn't being immoral or amoral in asking her to stay with him. There *was* a possible future for them!

Dear heaven! She had come so close to making the worst mistake in her life. If she hadn't followed the compulsion to read about Alyson, she would have left Sydney without ever knowing that she had every right to a chance of happiness with Dominic. As it was, she had kept him waiting for an answer for almost three weeks.

Carrie leapt to her feet and raced to the telephone, agitated at the thought that he might have given up because of her long silence. Her fingers trembled as she dialled the number Mrs. Coombe had written down for her. Her mind was a jumble of chaotic thoughts: fear, hope, need and deep desperate love all clamouring for expression.

The dragon's authoritative voice scythed through the chaos, wanting to know who was calling her. Carrie tried to calm herself, to speak rationally, to think how best to bridge the gap that she had created in her ignorance of Dominic's true marital status.

"It's Carrie Miller, Mrs. Coombe," she announced.

"Oh, my dear!" Authority cracked into instant anxiety. "What's wrong? What can I do?"

"Everything's fine, Mrs. Coombe," Carrie quickly assured her. "I was wondering if I might speak to Mr. Savage at some time. I know he's a very busy man, and there's no hurry, but I'd be grateful if you could let me know when it's convenient."

Silence.

"I don't want to interrupt anything," Carrie gushed on. "If you'd let me know when to call back...."

The dragon breathed some fire. "Priorities are priorities. Any call from you has top priority. And I know an *urgent* call when I hear one. Just hold on a second, my dear. I'll put you through immediately."

Carrie barely had time to recover from learning she was top priority in Dominic's busy world when his voice came on the line, sending a delicious rush of warmth right down to her toes.

"Carrie? What's wrong?"

"Dominic, I shouldn't intrude. There's nothing really wrong." She couldn't seem to get her thoughts in any order at all.

There was a strained alarm in his voice as Dominic tentatively filled in for her emotional confusion. "You're not disturbed by Dr. Burridge coming around, are you, Carrie? He didn't find anything wrong?"

"No. I'm a lot better. Didn't he tell you?" She rushed the words out.

There was a clearing of his throat. "Yes. You hadn't called, and I was worried."

"I'm sorry for leaving it so long, Dominic, but I..." She took a deep breath and plunged straight to the point of the call. "I've made up my mind. I would like to see you again... if you still wish to."

There was a moment of electric silence, then, "Carrie..." It was a bare, ragged whisper, like a half-strangled release of long-held control. "That would be wonderful," he added with definite fervour.

A wild dizziness whirled through Carrie's head. But it was not from any sick weakness. It was relief and joy and the turbulent release of all her long-repressed emotions. "I owe you so much. I thought...if you're free tonight, I could cook you dinner. It's the least I can do for—"

"I'm free. What time?"

A relaxed warmth pervaded his voice. Carrie had the immediate and strong sensation that if Dominic had not been free when she rang, he was now. He was good at cancelling appointments. For her. When she needed him. The fatuous smile on her face spilled into her voice.

"Whatever time suits you."

"Is six too early? I could leave the office as soon as I tidy things up and come straight over."

Suddenly words bubbled over each other. "Well, Danny and I usually have dinner at six-thirty, but—" She was going to add that six was fine. She didn't get the chance.

"Then six-thirty it is. I'll be there."

"Danny would like that. He loves the school, Dominic."

"Carrie, I don't want to put you to any trouble. I could take the three of us out to dinner."

"No. I want to cook for you, Dominic. Something special. It'll be my pleasure."

"And mine." There was a deep sigh. "I'll look forward to it, Carrie."

"So will I," she echoed with heartfelt feeling, then hung up as she felt tears pricking her eyes.

Maybe it was still madness to want him so much, she thought shakily. A mass of uncertainties started crowding in on her, tearing destructively at her newborn joy. Maybe Dominic wanted her out of some rebound effect from losing Alyson. His pride had to be hurt over his wife getting pregnant by another man.

Perhaps that was why he had frozen when she had called Danny her baby that first day...why he had wanted to take her home with him...why he had been thinking of his wife when Carrie had mentioned the gossip his actions would stir. There could hardly be anything more satisfying than parading a former lover around his home while Alyson was playing live-in lover to some magnate who was trying to recapture his youth. Tit for tat.

Dominic's desire for her had to be partly motivated by a need to retaliate, to wound his wife's pride by repeating a conquest that had niggled Alyson in the past.

Perhaps by pretending that it had always been Carrie he had really wanted, it made everything more acceptable to him. And she was right here, on hand, still obviously vulnerable to his attractions. It was so much easier for him to use her than to seek anyone new.

He might not have anything permanent in mind at all. Only another fling until he recovered from the wounds inflicted by Alyson.

With a fierce flash of resolution, Carrie quelled all the fears. It was stupidly self-defeating to be thinking along such negative lines. Dominic had to feel something for her. All she had to do was look at how much he had done for her and Danny. She couldn't believe it was only out of kindheartedness for underdogs, as Alyson had claimed. It had to be more than that. It might not be the kind of love she wanted, but it was something for her to build on.

She was no longer the inexperienced nineteen-year-old he had first met. She could hold her own in any sophisticated society now. She could show him tonight what a good hostess she was capable of being for him, if that was the kind of thing that was important to him. Which, given his position in the world, had to be. But over and above that, she would love him more than any other woman would. She had so much to give him if he really wanted her for always. At least she could try to make him want her for always... as she wanted him.

There was a chance that everything could work out.

Even the slimmest chance was better than nothing!

It meant so much, not only for her, but for Danny, as well.

Please, God, let it work out right, she prayed with almost feverish passion. Let him love me for what I am. Don't let me be deceived again. This means far too much. For everyone!

CHAPTER TEN

DOMINIC ARRIVED TEN minutes earlier than the agreed time of six-thirty. Carrie had just finished dressing in her favourite gold and beige sundress and was still in her bathroom brushing her hair when the buzzer went. It was Danny who admitted him to the apartment while Carrie tried to steady her fingers enough to apply some lipstick.

She didn't know whether it was apprehension or excitement that made her feel so nervous, but the moment she walked into the living room and saw Dominic again, the wild acceleration of her pulse left her in no doubt that she was in danger of losing her head as well as her heart.

Although he was early, he had obviously taken the time to change out of his business clothes. He wore superbly tailored grey slacks and a silk sports shirt patterned in navy and grey and white. Somehow his virile masculinity was even more pronounced in casual attire, and his whole image was less formidable and far too attractively approachable. Carrie's more intimate memories of him were instantly reawakened.

"Look what Mr. Savage has brought you, Mum!" Danny cried excitedly.

But she didn't need to look at the obvious courtship symbols—the sheaf of red roses, the box of imported chocolates, the bottle of Veuve Cliquot champagne. One look at Dominic was enough. His eyes told her what was on his mind as they clung to hers with compelling intensity, searching, wanting, stirring the response she could not hide from him any longer. He smiled, a slow smile of intense satisfaction.

"You look beautiful, Carrie," he said softly.

And somehow the years fell away, and it was just like that first smile he had given her at Jupiters Casino. She felt totally ravished by it.

"You do, Mum," Danny agreed with a cheeky grin. "You're not even skinny any more."

She gave a self-conscious laugh, aware that her skin had flushed with pleasure. She forced her legs forward, telling herself to appear graceful in every way. "You shouldn't have brought these gifts, Dominic. You make it so hard for me to return some of your generosity when you keep being more generous," she chided him with what she hoped was a charming smile.

"Just to be with you is more than enough return for me, Carrie," he said, his vivid blue eyes glowing with a warmth that heated her blood further.

Maybe it hadn't been a fantasy at all, she thought wildly. Maybe it had been as real as she had believed it was at the time—before Alyson and the others had turned it into something ugly—as real as it felt now. But she was so vulnerable to the desire. She *wished* to believe he truly cared for her, but she was not the only one who could be hurt by it this time. Carrie sternly warned herself to be cautious, to hold back until there was no shadow of doubt about Dominic's sincerity. She had to shield Danny from the kind of pain she had once suffered.

"I'll take these out to the kitchen and find a vase for them," she said as she took the roses.

"I'll come with you and open the champagne," Dominic quickly offered.

"Can I open the box of chocolates so that I can be of help, too?" Danny piped up.

"After dinner," Carrie replied, struggling to keep some command of her voice.

The next two hours proved a long struggle to keep command of anything. The many years of training provided an automatic control that stopped her from spoiling any part of the dinner she had prepared, but she didn't really taste a thing. Only Dominic's compliments on her cooking assured her that her efforts were successful. And very much appreciated.

Danny's presence helped to lend an air of normality to the evening. He chattered away to Dominic, claiming at least half of his attention. Carrie was intensely gratified by Dominic's interest in her son. There was not the slightest hint of condescension in his conversation. Indeed, it seemed to Carrie that he listened avidly to Danny's account of their life in Fiji as though he couldn't hear enough about it.

Occasionally what Danny told him evoked amusement, but quite often he flashed a look of pain at Carrie, as though the way they had lived caused him some inner distress. Of course, it had not been a life of material luxury—not the kind he was used to—but Carrie was quite proud of the way they had managed, and although Dominic didn't voice any criticism, she inwardly bridled against any adverse appraisal he might make of it.

On the whole, however, he was charming, and she couldn't take offence at anything for long. Eventually, of course, Danny's bedtime had to be announced. He then wanted to show off his new bedroom to Dominic. Carrie was quite happy to let them go off together while she stacked the dishwasher and made coffee.

It was a mistake that she very quickly regretted.

She had told Danny to get ready for bed and hadn't even considered the possibility that he might think of singing. The distinctive sound of his much-prized ukulele should have warned her, but she imagined Danny telling Dominic that it had been presented to him as a farewell gift by the Fijian staff on the island resort where they had last lived. However, her complacency was instantly dashed the moment she heard his clear child soprano voice lift into the traditional Fijian farewell song. *"Isa lei, na noqu rarawa..."*

A chill ran down her spine. She dropped everything and raced down the hallway to his bedroom. *"Danny!"* she almost shouted in her need to stop him.

His voice faltered as he took in her disapproving frown. "Dom asked me to sing it for him," he excused himself, bewildered by her vehemence.

"Dom?" It was Carrie's turn to look bewildered. Her gaze moved swiftly from the boy sitting cross-legged on his bed to the man who was sitting in the orange office chair swivelled around to face Danny.

"I told Danny he could call me that," Dominic explained, the blue eyes gently challenging her over his right to do so. Quite clearly his relationship with Danny was being fastened to a degree of intimacy that Carrie hadn't expected. Not this soon!

She tore her gaze from his, more worried about the other challenge he might make. "Danny, I told you it was your bedtime," she said reprovingly.

"Aw, Mum! Only a few minutes longer!" he wailed in protest. "Dom wanted me to sing *'Isa Lei.'* I was just telling him that I sang it for the boys in my class, and the teacher took me to the choirmaster during recess, and I had to sing it for him, too. He said he was going to put me in the school choir straight away."

"You didn't tell me that," Carrie said in some exasperation.

"It only happened today. I forgot about it until just now. I can't remember everything. I only just remembered the choirmaster said he hadn't heard a voice as good as mine since Dom was at school."

Carrie's heart stopped dead. She couldn't bring herself to look at Dominic.

"One chorus wouldn't hurt, would it?" Dominic put in mildly.

Carrie took a deep breath to calm her inner agitation. This scene was going way too fast for her, taking them right out into the middle of unknown depths. She had no idea where it might stop. Yet her fears and apprehensions could be unfounded. Dominic's mild tone of voice suggested nothing more than an interest to hear Danny sing. She had to make a decision, and to appear too adamant might arouse suspicions she had already laid to rest. She made up her mind.

"One chorus," she said sternly.

"And a verse," said Danny, and before she could contradict him, he was plucking out the tune on his ukulele.

It was the happiest of songs, and the saddest. So often through the long years it had filled her heart with ungovernable emotion and brought tears to her eyes. Somehow the words were inextricably linked to her brief relationship with Dominic, and even now she

automatically translated what Danny was singing in
Fijian.

Isa, Isa, you are my only treasure
Must you leave me, so lonely and forsaken
As the roses will miss the sun at dawning
Every moment my heart for you is yearning

Isa lei, the purple shadows fall
Sad the morrow will dawn upon my sorrow
Oh! Forget not, when you are far away
Precious moments beside Nanuya Bay.

Danny was obviously drawn by nostalgia to sing the
chorus one more time. Carrie couldn't stop him now.
The damage was done. And to compound matters,
Dominic joined in, singing *"Isa Lei"* in harmony,
humming the words he didn't know.

Carrie looked on in horror. Her worst fears were
being realised in front of her eyes. Dominic was not
only suffering the hurt of losing his wife, pregnant by
another man, but he was looking with more and more
yearning towards Danny. He really believed he had
found his son, and Carrie could not see any way of
laying that thought to rest now.

And where did that leave her? She didn't want
Dominic to want and love her because of Danny.
However selfish it was, she wanted Dominic to love
her for herself.

The last haunting note wafted wistfully into the air.
Carrie's eyes darted from one to the other, trying to
assess what each was feeling. Although Danny had
never voiced it, she knew he wanted a father figure—
that was only natural—and she certainly didn't mind

that person being Dominic. If their relationship was going to be permanent.

"That was beautiful, Danny," Dominic remarked quietly.

"Gee! I wish we could do that more often," came Danny's heartfelt desire. "Mum's great, but she can't sing a note."

"I can so," Carrie put in desperately.

"Not like Dom, Mum."

It was a fact she couldn't refute.

"I've got a guitar at home," Dominic slid in smoothly. "If you like, I could bring it next time I come, and we could all have a sing-along together."

"That would be super, Dom!" Danny enthused. "I'd love to learn guitar," he added without any subtlety whatsoever.

Dominic laughed. His eyes danced up at Carrie. "Well, if your mother says it's okay, I could teach you some. But she's the boss, Danny."

Relief poured through Carrie. Everything *was* all right. Dominic wasn't assuming anything he shouldn't.

"It's okay, isn't it, Mum?" Danny appealed eagerly.

"As long as you don't impose on Dominic, Danny. You mustn't ask for more than is offered," she gently chided.

Danny shot a worried look at Dominic. "I didn't mean you had to."

"It's okay, Danny. I'd like to," came the firm assurance.

Boy and man smiled happily at each other, their blue eyes mirroring an inner understanding that obviously gave them both the same kind of satisfaction.

"Bed," Carrie choked out huskily, moving forward to take the ukulele from Danny and lay it on the desk.

He was well content to snuggle down, cheerfully bidding them both good night. As he returned Carrie's kiss, he whispered, "Ask Dom around tomorrow night, Mum."

"We'll see," she murmured noncommittally. "Now be a good boy and go to sleep."

Dominic went ahead to the living room as Carrie turned out Danny's light and closed his bedroom door. She stood in the hallway for several moments, gathering her composure, telling herself it would not be wise to let things move too fast where she and Dominic were concerned. That was what she had done before. It behove her to tread more carefully this time.

She decided to get the coffee first. Then when she went into the living room, she would have something to do, and she wouldn't feel so tense, so aware of the intimacy that Dominic seemed intent on building between them. It was best to keep this a friendly social occasion, as far as possible. Only time could prove just how sincere Dominic was about wanting what he said he wanted.

When Carrie came in, bearing a tray that contained a plate of the special petit fours she had made, as well as the coffee things, Dominic was standing by the long windows, apparently viewing the city and harbour lights. He turned the moment he heard her step and stepped forward quickly to take the tray from her.

"No. It's all right, thanks," Carrie rushed out with a somewhat nervous smile. "Please . . . sit down and relax, Dominic."

He subsided onto one of the smaller sofas that flanked a long chesterfield. "I do like this suite you chose, Carrie," he remarked appreciatively. "Very comfortable."

"This is all Gina Winslow's work, Dominic," she hastily corrected him. "I didn't choose anything, really. Gina did ask me my preferences in style and colour, and somehow we always seem to agree on what would look best, but I honestly haven't pushed my ideas. I wouldn't do that."

A whimsical little smile flitted over his mouth. "Well, I must use Miss Winslow on more projects in future. She obviously has a fine touch."

"And amazingly efficient," Carrie added, delighted that Dominic was pleased with the new interior decoration and wanting to give Gina all the credit she deserved. "She's done all this so quickly. If it wasn't for the dining room suite being delayed two months, you'd have this apartment back in operation next week, Dominic, and I'd be off and out of your hair."

For some reason, that idea didn't meet with his approval at all. He frowned. "There's no hurry on it. In fact . . ." He hesitated, frowning even more heavily.

"You mustn't worry about me," Carrie put in quickly. "I'm quite well enough to get a job now."

He looked startled. "You mustn't even think of getting a job yet, Carrie," he protested vehemently. "You look well, but you're better off to take your time. It's just not worth the risk."

He leaned forward, his eyes stabbing at hers in urgent appeal. "And you're certainly not to consider moving from here. At least, not until . . . well, not until all the decorating's finished, anyway. And there'll probably be more holdups on that than Miss Winslow has anticipated. Only when it's all finished will it be time to consider a move somewhere else. I'm not about to put you out in the street. Surely you know I'd consider your needs ahead of anything else, Carrie."

It certainly seemed that way, but as much as it pleased Carrie to believe him, she was still wary of letting herself depend on him for too much. "I can support myself and Danny, Dominic," she said quietly. A flood of painful embarrassment scorched her cheeks as she forced herself to add, "Not to the standard you're accustomed to, but—"

"Don't, Carrie!" he broke in, his face twisting with anguish. "You've had it so hard all these years. I want to make it a little easier for you now. Please...it's bad enough, knowing what you've been through with no one to help."

"I had lots of help," she insisted, pride leaping to the fore once again. "The Fijians are the loveliest people on earth, particularly where children are concerned. Danny never wanted for loving minders whenever I needed them. And love and being loved is what living is all about. Danny never went short on that commodity. He's always been a happy child."

"And you? Were you happy all these years, Carrie?"

She dropped her gaze from his intense probe and set about pouring the coffee. "Some times have been happy. Some not," she stated evenly. "Life isn't exactly carefree when one has responsibilities."

"I would like to make your life carefree, Carrie," Dominic said softly.

She finished pouring the coffee, although how she managed not to spill any was a minor miracle. Then slowly she lifted her gaze, gently mocking the determined purpose she found burning in his. "That's not possible, Dominic. Because I'm not carefree. I do care. About a lot of things." She offered him a wry little smile. "But thank you for being so kind to me. And to Danny."

His mouth twisted in irony as he bent forward to stir sugar into the cup she had pushed towards him. "Danny's a fine boy, Carrie. You've done a marvellous job of raising him. I'd be very proud of him . . . if he were my son."

Her heart contracted. The temptation to confess the whole truth quivered on her tongue for several moments before she swallowed it back. One pleasant evening together was no test for what had to be a life-long commitment.

"I *am* very proud of him," she said stiffly.

Dominic seemed to stir his coffee forever before finally putting down the spoon and lifting his cup. His face looked tight. His eyes searched hers carefully before he spoke again.

"I'm looking forward to spending more time with him. You really don't mind about my suggesting the guitar?"

"Of course not. I used to love—" She was going to say when you played and sang to me, but she pulled herself up at the revealing phrase and self-consciously substituted other words. "Do you still enjoy playing?"

His grimace was self-mocking. "I'm afraid I let it slide years ago. Somewhere along the line I lost my joy in music."

Carrie frowned. "Then why make such an arrangement with Danny?"

The blue eyes caught hers in compelling need. "I want to try again, Carrie," he said softly. "I want to try a lot of things again. Things that I once cared about... very deeply. But without the right kind of people to share them ... they became meaningless."

Alyson could make anything meaningless, Carrie thought bitterly. She didn't understand, would never understand, why Dominic hadn't seen that for himself before making a marriage commitment with such a mean and despicable woman. But that was over now. Nothing could be gained by dwelling on the past. If she could give Dominic the future he wanted ...

She smiled. "I'm afraid Danny expects you to be super, Dominic. You'd better start practising again if you want to live up to his expectations."

He relaxed into a happy grin. "I'm sure I can manage enough chords to satisfy a seven-year-old. But I will practise. I don't intend to let my... singing partner down."

Carrie wasn't sure if she had imagined that slight pause in his speech or not. For one mind-stopping moment she had thought he was going to say "my son," but he had continued so smoothly that she decided it was her own supersensitivity on the point that had raised the spectre.

"You'll have to tell me when you're ready for a concert," she invited. "Danny would have you come again tomorrow night, but I guess that would be pushing it."

"Not at all," Dominic denied quickly. "If tomorrow night wouldn't be pushing it for you, I'm only too happy to oblige. Just say what suits you, Carrie. I don't want to impose on your hospitality."

"I enjoy cooking for an appreciative guest," she assured him. "But promise me you won't bring any more gifts."

"I'll try to restrain myself." His rueful smile suggested a double meaning that the sudden simmer in his eyes reinforced.

Carrie picked up her cup to cover the wild surge of desire that rushed through her body. Neither of them seemed to have anything to say while they drank their coffee. The silence lengthened, sharpening the physical awareness that Carrie had tried so hard to keep at bay. Her mind strove frantically to find another line of conversation. Something safe!

Dominic did not help.

His cup clattered on its saucer.

He stood up, tension screaming from every line of his body. "I think I'd better go, Carrie," he said stiffly.

Disappointment stabbed through her. She set down her cup in such a hurry it tipped over. She leapt up from the lounge, her body a mass of shrieking nerve ends, her mind a whirl of uncertainties. Her eyes sought his, desperately needing to know his feelings.

"I've enjoyed the evening, the company and the dinner very much," he said, as though forcing the words through a grimly held barrier of restraint. Then his face cracked into a rueful grimace. "I don't want to strain my welcome, Carrie."

"You couldn't, Dominic." The words spilled out artlessly, her need for him too pressing for any dissembling.

He made an awkward helpless gesture. She saw the struggle on his face. "Carrie . . . this means too much to risk putting any foot wrong. Alone with you I find I can't trust myself to behave as I know I must.''

"How must you behave?"

It was a crazy thing to ask—playing with fire—yet she couldn't stop herself from asking it. The desire he had been trying to suppress flared into his eyes. His chest expanded as he dragged in a deep breath. The battle for control went on.

"It's been a long wait, Carrie," he rasped. "I can wait a bit longer... until I've proved whatever it is I have to prove to you. So that you can trust me. If I go now then tonight's been all right, hasn't it?"

The note of desperation in his voice scoured Carrie's soul. "Yes." It was an explosion of her own pent-up feelings. "Yes," she repeated, but her eyes mirrored the uncontrollable need that was churning inside her, the need that so desperately wanted to be answered, the need that had been waiting so long, so very long....

"Carrie..." He stepped towards her, his hands lifting, reaching out, curling into fists, dropping. Anguish twisted across his face. He shook his head. "I must go. Thank you for... for letting me come."

"Dominic..."

It was a cry, straight from her heart, without any plan or thought, totally heedless of any consequence. She never knew afterwards if she stepped towards him at that critical moment. He had started to turn away from her. Her cry arrested the action. Their eyes locked, a raw aching desire leaping between them, compelling beyond any common sense or control, and the distance that separated them was abruptly and violently closed, the impact of their bodies so mind-shattering that all coherent thought ceased.

There was only feeling... Dominic's strong arms around her, crushing the softness of her body to the taut muscles of his... The heat of his mouth sweeping over her hair in a passionate flurry of kisses... The wild drumbeat of her heart, pounding its need to break through the heaving walls of their chests to reach his... Hands moving in feverish possessiveness... Heated flesh seeking heated flesh... Lips meeting, devouring, their mouths feeding the desire that yearned for more and more expression, that could never be satisfied with anything less than the total coming together that their bodies wanted.

"If this is wrong...I don't know what's right," Dominic groaned, his lips still sipping at hers. "Tell me, Carrie. Tell me you want this as much as I do."

"Yes..." There was no other response she could make. It was drawn from her soul, drawn from the dark well of loneliness that had ached to have this man, right or wrong....

And Dominic didn't wait for any other answer. He swept her off her feet and headed for her bedroom, driven by a need that couldn't bear to face up to questioning anything.

CHAPTER ELEVEN

PERHAPS IT WAS Dominic's breathing that woke Carrie from her light sleep. Her head was cradled on his shoulder, his arm curled around her, holding her firmly against his body. Even in sleep it did not seem that Dominic wanted to let go of her. It was a beautiful place to be, next to him, intimately coiled together. To Carrie, it was like coming home. Instinctively she felt it was the place she rightfully occupied, and always had.

They had made love so many times, her skin was highly sensitised to the slightest touch. The brushing of his legs against her own as he rolled onto his side was enough to arouse a leap of awareness, and she opened her eyes, instinctively wanting the wonderful intimacy they had shared to go on.

The morning light filtering through the curtains shocked her into another awareness. Her eyes darted to the bedside clock. Just past five. Danny didn't usually wake until about six-thirty. Carrie relaxed again, a sweet contentment curving her lips as she turned to the man who lay beside her.

Dominic...

His name was an exultant song inside her as her eyes roamed over the firm musculature of his shoulders and slid down the strong breadth of his chest to where the bed sheet lay loosely over his hips. He had always had a magnificent body, in Carrie's opinion, and just the sight of it excited her now. She gently lifted the sheet lower. She loved the firm swell of his bottom. It was perfect. And his powerfully muscled legs. She shivered with remembered pleasure as her gaze ran over his thighs, the sprinkle of dark hairs that had rubbed so deliciously against the satin smoothness of her skin.

She couldn't resist touching him. All last night it had been like opening a treasure trove that had been buried for years, all the contents known and loved, yet all the more precious and thrilling for having seemed lost but now found once more. Totally enthralling magic, and the reality of it—the sweet intense reality—had to be affirmed again and again. Even now, to feel the warmth of his skin, the slight contraction of his muscles as her fingertips slid over the erogenous zone just below his hip, the delicious fit of her hand around the firm curve of his buttock... her stomach twisted with the glorious pleasure of knowing he was hers to touch.

She leaned forward to kiss the vulnerable curve of his neck, and the tips of her breasts brushed his chest. Her nipples tingled into aroused excitement. With sheer sensual wantonness she rubbed them over his skin as her lips trailed to his shoulder and her hand glided forward, over his stomach.

With my body, I thee worship....

The words of the old marriage service slid through Carrie's mind, and she sighed in happiness at the thought of being married to Dominic. Having him like this, being with him, for always. He did love her. She was sure of it now. And she would make him see that she could be whatever he wanted in a wife. Not just in bed, but by his side in every capacity.

She suddenly found he was fully aroused. In the same moment of this discovery, Dominic's arm tightened around her, cuddling her closer, instantly drawing her gaze to his face. His blue eyes were wide open and glowing with pleasure. He smiled at her startled look.

"You can wake me like that any time, Carrie," he said, his voice furred with seductive sensuality.

She laughed a little self-consciously, happy that he was happy and that he could still desire her despite the excesses of the night, but at the same time realising that she was now bared to the light of day and her body could not bear the same scrutiny as his. There were faint stretch marks on her breasts and her stomach from her pregnancy, and she didn't want Dominic to see them.

"Is it time for me to go?" he asked, a trace of anxiety in his voice.

"Soon."

"How soon?"

"Danny rarely wakes before six."

He heaved a sigh of relief, checked his watch, then grinned at her. "That gives us plenty of time." He hitched himself up on the pillow and lifted a hand to stroke her hair away from her cheek and tuck it behind her ear. "I won't leave you until I absolutely have to," he stated, his eyes so warm and loving that heat tingled under her skin.

He bent his head and kissed her with tantalising lightness. Carrie lost all concern about her body and wound her arms around his neck, inviting him to take whatever he wanted of her. He kissed her again and again, teasingly sensual, slowly exciting them both towards the passionate hunger that simmered in both of them and needed so little fuelling to flare into compelling need.

His hand trailed down to her breasts and his palm revolved gently over the erect nipples, exciting them into a tight hardness. Carrie sucked in a quick breath as arrows of pleasure shot through her body. Her eyes clung to his, unable to hide the wanting, and the simmering desire in his was sharpened by a glitter of exultation.

"I love the feel of your breasts, Carrie," he murmured, slowly cupping the fullness in his hand. "So soft and womanly."

He shaped them to his mouth and hands, his tongue playing erotic dances around her nipples. Carrie felt herself drowning in the sweet pleasure of it. Slowly he increased the pressure, drawing on the sensitive flesh in a rhythm that sent fierce darts of sensation pulsing through her. She cried out as he built a tormenting need with his mouth. Her hands dragged through his hair and raked down to his shoulders. Her spine arched convulsively. He slid a hand between her thighs to soothe the aching desire for fulfilment.

"Dominic...please..." she moaned, as her body spun out of control.

He moved, carrying her with him as he rolled onto his back. "Take me, Carrie," he commanded, his eyes blazing with a fierce need, his hands supporting her quivering body, positioning her towards him. Slowly, tremulously, she absorbed his flesh within her own, and the heady excitement of seeing the expression on his face change, his eyes dilating, darkening, watching her with ever-deepening intensity, lent an exquisite awareness to the sensations spreading through her.

His hands glided lovingly over the soft curves of her body. "You are so exquisite, Carrie. The touch of you, the sight of you, the scent of you, the taste of you. To feel myself immersed in you like this...that's the greatest wonder of all."

All the love she had ever felt for him flowed through her like a tidal wave, and she could not, did not want to, deny him the words he had asked her to say weeks ago.

"I love you, Dominic."

"I know," he replied softly. There was a flash of fierce resolution in his eyes. "We will never be parted again. No matter what!"

A crest of exultant happiness bubbled into a delicious urge to tease him. "We can't stay locked together like this forever!"

A wicked delight sparkled back at her. "It seems like a great idea to me."

"Mmm..." she purred, trying an undulating movement with her hips.

Dominic sucked in a quick breath. His whole body went rigid for a moment. Then he grabbed her waist, pinning her to him as he swung her down on the pillows and took control, driving Carrie to a plateau of wildly pulsing sensation, faster, deeper, exciting a swirling tension that sent a tingling heat to her feet, her hands, her body, her brain, and just as she felt the spilling heat of his climax, her whole body spasmed in response, seeming to melt with a gushing joy around him.

He hugged her close for a long time afterwards, rubbing his cheek over her hair, stroking her back in long, sensual caresses. Finally he tilted her face up to his and kissed her with a sweet fervour that curled its loving reassurance around her heart.

"It's time, Carrie," he murmured. "I guess I should be leaving now."

"Yes." She sighed in reluctant resignation. "Thank you, Dominic."

He gave her a rueful little smile. "It hurts, but I wouldn't do anything that would distress you. And there is the promise of tonight."

"Yes." She smiled back, her eyes rewarding his caring with a deep glow of appreciation. "Don't forget to bring your guitar."

He laughed and dropped a kiss on her nose. "You are the music of my life," he said, then gently disentangled himself to get out of bed. "And I'll remind you of that tonight. With guitar and without it," he tossed at her as he headed for the bathroom.

Carrie sat up and hugged her knees, feeling so happy she could burst from it. Her eyes roved around the lovely bedroom that Gina had decorated for her, newly delighted by everything she saw, the elegant curtains in the lemon and apricot and pale green floral, with their apricot sashes and piping; the armchairs in the same fabric with the apricot silk cushions leaning against the armrests; the pale green lamps with the fluted apricot lamp shades; the magnificent secretary, which had to be a terribly expensive antique; the matching side tables; the chevalier mirror—Carrie loved everything.

And now she could stay here.

Dominic wanted her to stay here.

At least until... She remembered Dominic's pause before he added about the decorating being finished. He had meant until their relationship was settled.

Carrie was certain of that now. After all, he had wanted to take her to his home at first, and she suspected that was what he really wanted. But he was being careful not to rush things, to make sure it was right with her. And she was glad of that. She wasn't prepared to move into Dominic's home unless he was prepared to marry her.

He hadn't yet talked about marriage, only about not being parted again. Carrie sternly told herself to be patient about that. She had to show him that she could make him a suitable wife. At the present moment he could very well be shy of marriage anyway, after the disaster with Alyson. Besides, his divorce wasn't through yet. At least time was on her side in this new situation.

The question she really needed to have answered was the one that had tortured her over the years, and even more so lately. What had Dominic seen in Alyson Hawthorn that had made him choose to marry her?

It didn't really make sense that money and property had influenced his choice of wife. Surely Dominic's family had been wealthy and prestigious enough not to require a merger with another well-established family.

Carrie conceded that a similar background and social standing did make for an easier understanding between two people, but to her mind, Dominic's character and personality had been so different to Alyson's. On the other hand, it was probably true enough that opposites attract. Yet Dominic hadn't actually shown any great attraction towards Alyson.

It seemed to Carrie that there had to be something Alyson had—some particular quality that Dominic had seen as of special value to him in a marriage.

Something that had typified Alyson as wife material, over and above an emotional love he felt for anyone else.

And if that was the case, Carrie needed to find out what it was so that she could cultivate it. It was not just idle curiosity. She had a real need to know. Now that she had another chance with Dominic, she did not want him to find any shortcomings in her, or in their togetherness.

He came out of the ensuite bathroom, freshly washed and shaven, and he looked so splendid that Carrie's train of thought was completely lost.

He gave her a rueful grin. "Keep looking at me like that, Carrie, and all my good intentions will fly out the window. You're far too tempting, my love."

She laughed and pulled the sheet up over her breasts and tucked it under her arms.

"I'm not sure that's any better," he complained.

"I think you should get dressed and stop flaunting yourself at me," Carrie retorted in kind.

He laughed, enjoying the relaxed atmosphere between them, then set about picking his clothes up from the floor.

Carrie took great pleasure in watching him dress. Somehow it lent an extra intimacy to all that had gone before. It would be like this every morning if they were married, she thought. Or did Dominic only want them to be lovers?

That uncertainty lingered in her mind, prompting the question about Alyson. Carrie hesitated. Perhaps she should wait. She had the feeling that she might be opening a Pandora's box of troubles that was better left shut. If Dominic had been deeply hurt by his marriage, it would be foolish of her to remind him of it.

Yet if he loved her... And after last night, could he possibly care about Alyson any more? The need to know pressed the decision. And she had already waited so patiently for so long, trying not to hurt anyone, that for once her own need came first.

"Dominic..."

He looked up from tucking his shirt into his trousers and smiled, the blue eyes bright with anticipation of whatever she might say to him.

Carrie took a deep breath. "There's a question I'd like to ask you. If you don't want to answer it, it doesn't matter," she added hastily, apprehensive about spoiling the mood between them.

"Ask away," he invited blithely.

"Well... would you mind telling me..."

She wasn't aware that her green eyes were filling with vulnerable appeal, but she felt tension streaking along all her nerves. Dominic looked at her quizzically as she hesitated again. Carrie ended up blurting the question out in a rush.

"What did you find so attractive about Alyson Hawthorn, Dominic?"

His hands stilled. His whole body seemed to be poised in utter stillness. His face was frozen in an expression of shock. Carrie's mind screamed at her that she had made an awful mistake. The past was the past. It was stupid, stupid, stupid to drag it up when the future beckoned so brightly.

The shock on his face slowly faded into dawning comprehension, a comprehension that seemed to appall him. "Carrie..." His voice was a harsh rasp. His throat moved in a convulsive swallow. "What made you think I found Alyson Hawthorn attractive?"

Her heart felt as though it was tumbling over itself. Bewilderment was followed by a painful storm of confusion. "Well, there had to be some reason..." The look on Dominic's face made it clear that whatever he had felt for Alyson was long gone. "I shouldn't have asked. I'm sorry. It doesn't matter."

"It does matter!" He advanced towards her, the blue eyes probing with an intensity that carried a blazing need to draw answers from her. He sat on the bed beside her and took hold of her shoulders, forcing her to look up at him. "Carrie, I know this is important. You have to tell me."

Her confusion grew worse. This was all the wrong way around. It was *he* who had to tell *her*. She shook her head. She should have waited.

"Please, Carrie...tell me one reason you thought I found Alyson attractive."

The urgency in his voice only served to heighten the unreality of what was going on. Carrie couldn't understand him. Never would. She tried to get the circling chaos into a straight line. "I could never understand what you saw in her," she said dully, wishing he would just answer her or let the subject drop.

"And if I said I saw nothing at all?"

Her eyes filled with pained accusation. Why was he trying to deceive her now? What point was there in it? Why couldn't he just give her the truth? That part of their lives was over. He didn't have to cover up and turn it into something different. All she had wanted was to understand. Surely it wasn't asking much for him to tell her.

"Then why did you marry her, Dominic?" she demanded, forcing him out of all evasion.

She felt the gasp of air hit his lungs. Horror and disbelief were stamped on his face. "Marry her!" The words came from his lips in violent rejection. "Marry that sly manipulative bitch? Carrie, I wouldn't have touched Alyson Hawthorn with a bar of soap, let alone..."

His head jerked in anguished denial. His hands lifted from her arms in a gesture of helpless appeal. He rose from the bed and paced around in extreme agitation.

Carrie watched him in a daze of spiralling shock. "You didn't marry her?" She forced the words from the mess that was her mind.

"No!"

The explosive negative completely shattered any equilibrium she had left. She stared at him, trying to steady herself, trying to take in the implications of this revelation. He must have changed his mind about marrying Alyson. And if he wasn't married to her, he was not getting a divorce from her.

"You married someone else," Carrie said, and the words seemed to come from a great distance. Her ears had a strange ringing in them.

"Carrie..."

It sounded like a protest. She saw his struggle to bring himself under control. The strain showed clearly on his face, but the observation only registered at the dimmest edge of her mind. He came to the bed and sat down, taking her hands this time, his fingers rubbing roughly over them as if seeking to reach under her skin. His eyes held an agonised plea.

"Yes, I did marry someone else," he acknowledged. "I'm sorry if that hurts you. Her name was Sandra Radcliffe. She wasn't there that summer. As far as I know, you never met her."

His face was tinged with hopelessness. Somehow he knew how important this was to her, but with their differing attitudes towards love and commitment, it was also clearly impossible for him to know why. Even to Carrie, the implications were only starting to sink in.

"It doesn't matter," she said defensively. "I shouldn't have asked." But she knew it did matter and couldn't keep the despair from her voice.

The words rushed from him, trying to bridge the gap of years that had been so suddenly shattered like fine crystal, the shards stabbing out in all directions. "Please understand, Carrie...."

She could hear the note of pleading in his voice and she did want to understand. She desperately wanted to. So she gave him all the attention she could muster.

"I'd spent years trying to find you, and I'd finally given up hope. Life was so empty...lonely...and then I met Sandra. I didn't love her as I love you. Never did. But I was thirty by then. And I did want children."

He didn't realise that the timing of his marriage—or the reason for it—didn't matter at all. The inexorable truth was that Dominic wasn't free. He had a wife. And Carrie had been a party to committing adultery all night. She hadn't known that. There was no wilful intent behind what had happened. She wasn't really guilty of taking another woman's husband. But it had happened.

She dully remembered that Dominic had meant to leave without touching her. He had even admitted it was wrong... although it felt right.

But it wasn't right!

It could never be right.

He was married to another woman.

"As it turned out, Sandra couldn't have children," Dominic continued sadly. "But she needed me, Carrie...."

"Of course," she whispered. Her mouth had gone completely dry. "I understand, Dominic."

She understood perfectly. Any woman married to Dominic would need him. For the rest of her life. And she certainly understood his desire now for Danny to be his son. But she couldn't bear to hear him talk about his wife. Not when the memory of their illicit intimacy was pulsing so painfully through her heart.

"I think you'd better go now. It's getting late," she said flatly.

He frowned. "About Alyson, Carrie..."

"I had a wrong idea about Alyson. That's all," she cut in quickly. Strange how her mind could work on a level that sounded quite sane and sensible while her whole bright new world was crumbling into ruins around her. "And now I know it was wrong. I don't want to go on about it. I'd rather you dropped the whole subject, Dominic. I feel enough of a fool as it is."

Conflict chased across his face, the need to pursue his own interests battling against her plea for forbearance. Frustration and disappointment finally gave way to reluctant resignation. "You just want to go on from here. Is that it, Carrie?" he asked softly.

"Yes," she said on a rush of sheer relief. She would have said anything to stop him involving her in a discussion about his marriage. Just the thought of that other woman who couldn't have his children waiting at home for him...

"I didn't mean to upset you." His eyes searched hers anxiously, obviously wanting to put everything right between them before he left. "Believe me, I'm content just to have you again, Carrie. Any way I can."

Her whole body ached for the contentment she had just lost. "Yes," she agreed. It was the easiest word to say. Her conscience accused her of having said it far too much lately, where Dominic was concerned.

"Then I'll see you tonight," he said, and leaned forward to kiss her goodbye.

She knew she shouldn't respond to it, but a terrible surge of despair gripped her heart, and before she knew what she was doing, she had flung her arms around his neck and was kissing him back as though her very life depended on it.

When Dominic finally lifted his mouth from hers, he shook his head wryly and drew in a deep breath. "Tonight," he said, as though he needed to repeat the promise of what was to come before he could force himself to go. He stroked her cheek in a last tender salute. "Tell Danny I'll bring my guitar."

Carrie nodded, too choked up to speak.

Dominic smiled and left, shutting her bedroom door very quietly behind him, careful not to make any noise that might wake Danny before he could depart.

Carrie sat staring at the closed door for a long time, her heart fighting fiercely against her conscience. She could let that door open again and keep Dominic in her life . . . be his kept woman on the side. And maybe he would divorce his wife eventually and marry her.

And maybe he wouldn't . . . if he could have her any way he wanted. His wife needed him.

Besides, how could she be a party to hurting a woman who was innocent of any wrongdoing? Who had married Dominic in good faith and had every right to have that good faith returned. While Carrie had no rights at all . . . except Dominic's love for her, and her love for him.

There was a rap on the door and Danny's voice piping behind it. "Mum, are you awake?"

"Just a minute!"

She scrambled from the bed, scooped up her clothes that had been so heedlessly discarded last night, threw them into a cupboard and quickly dragged a housecoat over her nakedness.

What about Danny's rights? she cried inwardly, as she opened the door to her son. But she knew that that was no argument. It had never been an argument. She would not use her child to force anything from Dominic. Especially not now.

Danny's vivid blue eyes sparkled up at her. "Did you ask him, Mum?"

She frowned, struggling to drag her mind off its inner torment. "What, Danny?"

"Dom. To come tonight. With his guitar."

The eagerness in his face twisted Carrie's heart. Was it right to keep a boy from his father? Wasn't a part-time father better than no father at all? Dominic could be so good for him.

"He has other commitments, Danny," she temporised.

"Oh!" His face fell in disappointment.

And how many other disappointments would we have, when Dominic had to be with his wife? What excuse had Dominic given for his absence last night? What excuse would he think of for tonight? When would he start making excuses to her and Danny? How long would he be a part-time father to Danny?

Carrie shook her head. She couldn't live with that situation. It was just as well she had held her tongue last night. Better for Dominic not to know that Danny was his son. Better for Danny not to know that Dominic was his father. Maybe they could just be friends . . . given time.

Carrie savagely mocked that thought.

It was no answer to her dilemma.

But she had to find an answer.

Before tonight.

CHAPTER TWELVE

JUST FOR ONCE, luck was on her side.

The answer was delivered in the mail.

It came in the form of a reply to one of Carrie's job applications. A positive reply. She was offered the position of top cook in a motel restaurant at Mudgee. Accommodation was provided. A telephone number was given. Would she call and confirm arrangements? The management needed her quickly and desperately. They wanted her to take up the job as soon as possible.

It meant she could once more be completely independent. She had somewhere to go, somewhere to live, and she would be earning an income that would support her and Danny. She was in a hopelessly compromising position here in the APIC company apartment, with Danny attending a school for which Dominic had paid the fees—albeit without her knowledge or permission. With this job, she could pay him back all that was owed. In money terms, anyway.

As much as it broke her heart to leave Dominic again, especially after last night, if he was really prepared to make a life with her and Danny, the choice was open to him. Even though it was a terrible choice to make, and someone was bound to be hurt.

He could get out of his marriage, or he could stay with it.

If he decided on the latter, then she and Danny were better off on their own. Part-time love without total commitment was not something she could ever be really content with.

She called the Mudgee motel and accepted the position. The manager told her what train she could catch from Sydney. She said she would be on tomorrow's train. She did not intend to walk out on Dominic without a word this time. She fiercely wished she hadn't all those years ago. Dominic had changed his mind about marrying Alyson Hawthorn. He said he had loved her—always had—and only married someone else because he had given up hope of ever finding her again.

If that was the case, if he asked his wife for his freedom, Carrie would wait for him. And she really meant *wait*. There would be no more lovemaking until Dominic was free. Otherwise...well, she had to tell him she could not accept any other kind of future with him. It wasn't right. And never could be right.

She was in the midst of packing when the buzzer announced a visitor. Carrie immediately assumed it must be Gina and went to admit her. She was startled when the dragon announced herself. What was Mrs. Coombe doing here in the middle of a working day? Carrie had put a stop to the shopping visits weeks ago. Nevertheless, she could hardly refuse her entry. The woman had been kind in her own authoritative fashion.

Carrie waited in the lobby, hoping to head off any further interference from Dominic's secretary. Mrs. Coombe stepped out of the elevator carrying a guitar case. She bestowed a benevolent smile on Carrie.

"Hello, my dear. My goodness, you have had an amazing effect on Mr. Savage!" The grey eyes actually twinkled. "Bringing a guitar to his office and singing! I've never seen him so happy! He had to go off for a conference at Peppers, up in the Hunter Valley, and he said to drop the guitar off with you to save him coming back to the office. But he won't be late, dear. The helicopter will be waiting to whiz him back to Sydney."

Carrie was so taken aback, as well as being highly embarrassed by this uncharacteristic burst of confidences from the dragon, that she didn't have wits enough to stop the formidable lady from charging into the living room and leaning the guitar case against one of the sofas.

"Oh, this is nice!" The steely grey eyes swept around, not missing any detail of Gina's decorative genius. Carrie got another smile, a veritable beam of approval. "So comfy and pleasant. I do admire your taste, dear."

Carrie heaved an impatient sigh. "It's Miss Winslow's work, Mrs. Coombe. I had nothing to do with it."

The dragon made a click of annoyance with her tongue. "Of course! Well, I must say she's done a marvellous job. Would you mind if I had a little peek in some of the other rooms?"

Since Mrs. Coombe was the top executive secretary at APIC and probably had the responsibility of arranging accommodation for clients, Carrie felt she had no option but to accede to the request.

"Of course I don't mind." The buzzer rang again and Carrie seized on the excuse not to accompany her.

"Please excuse me, Mrs. Coombe. You go right ahead and look all you want."

It was Gina, and Carrie was only too pleased to admit her. Apart from being spared the dragon's undiluted company, she wanted to say goodbye to her friend and tell her how pleased Dominic had been with her work. It was always a pleasure to have one's talents and hard work praised, and Gina certainly deserved every accolade going. She was a super person, apart from anything else.

However, the moment she stepped out of the elevator, Gina wrinkled her pert nose in good-humoured frustration. "Bad news, I'm afraid. You know I told you the dining room suite would be two months away. Well, there's been a further delay on materials, Carrie, and they won't guarantee a time for delivery. We're just going to have to wait and see."

"It doesn't matter to me, Gina," Carrie assured her, "although I am sorry you're being held up on the job. Oddly enough, Dominic—Mr. Savage—said only yesterday that you'd probably run into more delays."

"Is that a fact?" Gina said with a crooked little smile.

"Yes. And he thought you'd done a brilliant job so far. He even said he'd be considering employing you for other projects."

The crooked smile turned into a grin of dazzling proportions. "I sure would like that, Carrie. This job has been an absolute dream!"

"Are you rushing, Gina, or have you got time for a cup of coffee?" Carrie pressed anxiously.

"Coffee would go down very well," came the feeling reply. "I've been dashing around all morning."

They moved towards the kitchen, only to be halted by the sight of the dragon, charging down the hallway with the light of battle in her eyes, her bosom heaving as though she was stoking the engine room for the fire to be breathed.

"What is the meaning of all this packing?" she demanded to know.

Carrie grimaced. It was none of Mrs. Coombe's business, but that was obviously no consideration in her mind. She had the bit by the teeth and was in no mood to be fobbed off. Carrie decided there was little point in evading the issue. Dominic had already left the office for his conference and would be coming here straight afterwards. What did it matter if the dragon was told before he was? It didn't change anything.

"I'm packing because I'll be leaving here in the morning, Mrs. Coombe," she stated evenly.

"Leaving!" The Dragon and Gina chorussed in unison, each with the same note of appalled horror.

Carrie frowned at both of them, bewildered by their vehement reaction. "You know that my being here was only a temporary arrangement. I've got myself a job somewhere else, with live-in accommodation."

Carrie didn't want to tell them where. She had images of Dominic following her because he couldn't have what he wanted. If she had to cut free of him, better to do it cleanly, as she had in the past.

"You *can't* take a job somewhere else!" the dragon puffed in righteous indignation.

Carrie was beginning to feel a bit angry herself. This really was no one's business but her own. "I have the right to do anything I want, Mrs. Coombe," she stated sharply.

That took some of the steam out of the dragon, but she eyed Carrie with stern censure. "You really are the most ungrateful creature I've ever met!"

"Me? Ungrateful?" Carrie could hardly believe her ears. "To whom? How have I ever been ungrateful?"

Mrs. Coombe drew herself up in formidable authority. The grey eyes glittered intense disapproval. "When Mr. Savage went to the expense of buying this apartment for you, and having it decorated entirely to your taste—"

"Mrs. Coombe, you are totally and terribly wrong!" Carrie broke in, appalled that Dominic's secretary should have leapt to such conclusions. "In your position you should know better. This apartment is not for me. It's owned by APIC and it's used for the company executives and their associates and clients."

There! Take that, Carrie thought belligerently. They were Dominic's exact words.

The dragon snorted smoke. "APIC has nothing to do with this. The company has never bothered with any such thing."

"Truly!" Carrie argued vehemently. "You just don't know."

"I? Not know?" Eyebrows shot up in haughty scorn. "My dear girl, I have been in the confidence of Mr. Savage, and his father before him, for over twenty years. There is nothing I don't know!"

"Well, you're wrong about this!" Carrie returned stubbornly, refusing to submit to sergeant-major bully tactics.

"I most certainly am not! There was an extreme penalty clause in the contract Mr. Savage had to sign for it. If settlement of the contract was delayed and not affected within six weeks of exchange, he had to pay many thousands of dollars a week in punitive damages. All to have this apartment immediately available so he could move you into it that very day! Even the agents found it stunning and inexplicable. It was one of the worst deals Mr. Savage has ever made in his life. Simply because it had to be done so quickly. *For you!*" she finished triumphantly.

Carrie stared at her in stunned disbelief. "You've got to be joking," she murmured weakly.

It earned a disdainful snort. "I've never made a joke in my life! Not for any reason! Never!" The sergeant-major swung her unshakable authority onto Gina. "Tell Miss Miller your instructions from Mr. Savage!" she commanded.

"Mrs. Coombe..." Gina fidgeted. Her eyes swung warily from one antagonist to the other. "I can't do that," she began uncertainly. "I gave my word to Mr. Savage."

"Please do as you're told. In this matter, I speak for Mr. Savage himself," Mrs. Coombe said in her best no-nonsense voice. "I chose you in the first place. I'm now ordering you, on Mr. Savage's behalf. So do as I tell you or the consequences—believe me—will be that you will never work for APIC again," the sergeant-major threatened.

Gina turned troubled eyes to Carrie, but Mrs. Coombe's threat was sufficient. Her mind had been made up for her in no uncertain terms. "It's true...all of it. My brief, from Mr. Savage, was to ascertain what you liked and do my best to please you with all the furnishings. He wanted you to be happy here, to have all the things you would love. Cost was to be no object. Anything at all you fancied. I was to get it for you one way or another. But I had to be careful not to let you realise that it was all being done especially for you. And I had to do it quickly so you'd be completely comfortable as soon as possible. Except for one important piece of furnishing that I had to hold back on.''

"The dining room suite," Carrie murmured numbly.

"Yes. Mr Savage called me this morning and told me to make the delay a lot longer." Gina heaved a rueful sigh. "I'm sorry that it was kind of deceiving you, Carrie, but I couldn't see any harm in it. And you have been happy with what I've done. I've really enjoyed working with you. Giving you the pleasure Mr. Savage wanted you to have. And just being with you. Please believe that."

"Yes," Carrie whispered, too dazed to question what anyone said any more. She sat down on the nearest sofa and tried to make sense of all that Dominic had done for her. *Cost no object...* From the time he had left her that first afternoon, before he had even seen Danny, or suspected that her son might be his. He had done all this, set it all up, spent thousands and thousands of dollars, more . . . just for *her!*

"Why?" she murmured. It was so insanely extravagant. Her eyes lifted to the dragon, blindly seeking answers. "How could he do it?" Particularly when she had fought against any further involvement with him, Carrie thought, trying to absolve herself of any blame. For Dominic to just go ahead and . . .

"When Mr. Savage sets out to do something, he does it!" the dragon informed her categorically. "As to why, surely that's as obvious as the nose on my face." She sniffed for good measure, showing her nose in all its majesty. "Even if you don't love *him,* at least you could show some small smidgen of gratitude."

"Mrs. Coombe..." All the anguish of mind and heart that had wracked Carrie since early this morning poured into her voice. "What about his wife?"

"What about his wife?" came the wrathful retort. "That ended nearly two years ago. At the same time as his father died. Do you realise how crippling it is to have the two people closest to you die at almost the same time?"

It was a rhetorical question. She didn't expect a reply to it. Nor did she get one. Carrie simply stared at her, rendered totally speechless as revelations gushed from the dragon's mouth like an endless stream of fire, scorching away any possible objections Carrie might have to Dominic's interest in her.

"There's been more than a decent mourning period for Sandra. Surely to heaven you can't begrudge him some happiness now. After all he's been through, what with his father, then Sandra...and you looking so thin and ill that he was afraid you might have cancer, too.... And the grief that caused him... And then you refusing to go to hospital. Or see doctors. Taking the same wilful self-destructive attitude Sandra did..."

"His wife... Sandra...she died?" It was the one important fact to come out of Mrs. Coombe's torrent of indignation. Other things she could think of later, but a dreadful pressure was lifting off Carrie's brain, and her heart was already leaping with a surge of wild strength.

The dragon frowned her displeasure at Carrie. "Of course she's dead. Don't you know the first thing about Mr. Savage? He is the most honourable man I know. In business and out of it. Are you so ignorant

not to even realise that Mr. Savage would never interest himself in another woman if he had a wife? And
there's few men I can say that for!''

"I thought..." Carrie dragged in a deep breath and
expelled it in a long shuddering sigh of sweet relief.
"I've made the most terrible mistake."

"You certainly have!" A finger shot out and
wagged sternly at Carrie. "That man deserves some
consideration. From you. A great deal of consideration. If there's one thing I can't stand it's base ingrat-
itude. And it's about time you gave him something
back instead of pursuing your own selfish desires. Instead of going on with this harebrained idea of getting a job and leaving, you could begin by saying
thank you, and then—"

"Oh, I will, Mrs. Coombe. I will!" Carrie cried,
and startled the old lady into spluttering silence by
springing up from the sofa and hugging her and kissing her on the cheek. She wasn't a dragon after all. A
good watchdog, maybe, but not a dragon. And Carrie could have hugged her for a lot longer, but she
wasn't sure Mrs. Coombe's dignity would stand for
that. As it was she was ruffled into helpless bewilderment.

"You will what?" she asked.

"Give Mr. Savage a lot of consideration. And show
him some gratitude," Carrie burbled.

"Well...so you should."

"And I'm terribly grateful to you for explaining it
all to me," Carrie said with deep sincerity.

Mrs. Coombe recovered her usual composure. "Not
at all. What has to be done, has to be done. And I'm
the person to do it." She eyed Carrie sternly. "Just
don't let Mr. Savage know what I've told you. That

was at my discretion. Of which I have a lot. But Mr. Savage might not appreciate it straight away. Men can sometimes be very difficult in matters of pride.''

"And, uh, Carrie..." Gina chimed in. "If you don't mind, I'd rather him not know that I spilled the beans, too. I mean ... well, I'd really like to get into more of Mr. Savage's projects ... with Mrs. Coombe's help.''

In a flood of emotion, Carrie gave her a hug, too. "Don't worry about a thing. You have my promise. And thanks for making a beautiful home for me, Gina.''

She laughed and hugged her back. "You've been the easiest client I've ever had, Carrie. A dream job. And let me tell you, if I had a guy like Dominic Savage wanting to make me happy, I'd grab him fast and never let him go.''

"It's not quite as easy as that," Carrie said ruefully. "There are things between us...."

Like confessing the truth about Danny. And explaining why she had not told him before. She couldn't just go on from here, even if Dominic was content to do so. The past had to be cleared away. And that could not be done in front of her son.

She swung back to Mrs. Coombe, her eyes filling with anxious appeal. "May I ask you one more favour?''

"I'll do what's necessary, at my discretion. But if I can help in this situation, I will." Mrs. Coombe's stern demeanour was softening.

"It's Danny. I want to be alone with Mr. Savage for a while. If it could be arranged...''

"I'll pick Danny up from school and take him to a late afternoon screening of a film. Then we'll have hamburgers and chips. My boys always loved doing

that. Don't you worry about him. We'll enjoy ourselves immensely. I'll bring him home at seven. Is that
time enough?''

"If it's not too much trouble," Carrie breathed in
grateful relief. "You are a real treasure, Mrs. Coombe.
Thank you so much."

"Not at all." She brushed Carrie's words off, but
her face actually glowed with pleasure. "Mr. Savage
has a very nice voice. He should sing more often."

She cleared her throat and addressed Gina in her
sergeant-major voice. "Miss Winslow, we'd better be
going. You have a lot to do. You have to speed up the
dining room suite now that we all understand one another. And change anything Miss Miller would like
changed. But that part can wait until tomorrow. Miss
Miller won't have time to discuss such things today."

The grey eyes fixed their command onto Carrie
again. "You have a lot to do. Those job arrangements have to be immediately cancelled, and everything unpacked again and put away, and, uh, getting
yourself ready for Mr. Savage's visit."

"You're right, Mrs. Coombe," Gina agreed, but
there was a wicked twinkle in the eyes she turned to
Carrie. "Lots of considerations."

A lot more than Gina could ever imagine, Carrie
thought, a nervous flutter starting up in her stomach.
But it had to work out right in the end. It just had to.
Dominic loved her. More than she had ever dreamed.
And she loved him.

And there was Danny. . . their son. Dominic had to
be told. However unpleasant the consequences might
be from the explanations she had to give, there was no
way to avoid telling the whole truth now. She owed it

to Dominic. And much much more. If he could find it in his heart to forgive her, to understand...

It was a risk she had to take anyway. There was no way around it, and Carrie didn't want a way around it. Only the truth would serve their future happiness now.

CHAPTER THIRTEEN

FORTUNATELY THE MANAGER of the Mudgee Motel had another applicant for the position Carrie had to refuse. Carrie hated letting anyone down, but Dominic had her first consideration and always would from now on.

Unpacking did not take long.

Carrie wasn't sure when Dominic would arrive. Most probably he would think she expected him at six-thirty, like last night, but she willed him to come earlier. She needed far more than half an hour alone with him.

Since Danny would not be having dinner with them, and she remembered that Dominic liked Italian food, she prepared a special lasagne, which could be popped into the oven anytime. She couldn't make up her mind what to wear, finally deciding it didn't matter. Dominic loved her anyway. She prayed that he would still love her, despite what she had to tell him.

Alyson had more than lied to her. Mrs. Coombe had insisted that Dominic was an honourable man, and an honourable man wouldn't have made love to her if he was engaged to marry someone else. She hoped Dominic could forgive her lack of faith in his love, that he would understand what she had done and why. If only she had waited for him that day. She had been such a fool not to have given him a hearing before she left, to have let her mind be poisoned by that lying bitch of a woman instead of listening to her heart.

All the wasted years.

The pain.

Alyson had cheated all of them.... Dominic, herself and Danny. Carrie asked herself why? Maybe Alyson just couldn't bear anyone else to be happy, to be in love, and she had been jealous because of what Dominic and she had shared. What had she said—"gooey green eyes"? But in the end, Alyson had only succeeded in her cruel manipulation because Carrie had not believed enough! She hadn't believed that Alyson could be so evil, and she hadn't believed that Dominic could have such friends if he didn't share their attitudes, and she hadn't believed he truly loved her... as she loved him.

Carrie was still churning between guilt and hope and fear and despair and desperate love when Dominic turned up. It was just past five-thirty as he stepped out of the elevator, and all Carrie's turbulent emotions crystallised into one pure beam of overwhelming love. He had come... He was here for her, the man she had wanted to have with her for so long. She threw herself into his arms and hugged him so tightly that Dominic was startled.

"Carrie? What's wrong?" he asked anxiously, his hands automatically moving to soothe any distress.

"I just love you so much, Dominic," she breathed huskily, revelling in the scent of him, the feel of him, the caring he had always shown her. Always.

He gently tilted her head and smiled at her, the blue eyes shining with a deep blaze of happiness. "I'm so glad you can say that, Carrie. Right up until last night I was afraid I was going to lose you again. It sure is a good feeling to know that everything's all right."

But it wasn't. Not yet. And he saw the inner disquiet flit over her face. "Something is wrong, isn't it?" He frowned, his eyes suddenly darting to the living room. "Where's Danny?"

She eased back a little from his embrace and screwed her courage to the sticking point. "He's gone to a film with Mrs. Coombe, Dominic. I asked her to mind him. I want to talk to you alone."

He tensed and looked even more concerned. "Carrie, if you're worried about anything, we can work it out."

"I hope so, Dominic," she said fervently. "Come in and sit down," she pressed, linking her arm around his and drawing him into the living room. "Would you like a drink?" she asked, nerves playing havoc with her resolution.

"Not right now, thanks, Carrie. I'd rather hear what you want to say first."

He was right. No point in prolonging the agony. She saw him settled on one of the sofas, but found her inner agitation too great to sit down herself. She wandered over to the windows before forcing herself to turn and face him.

"I haven't been fair to you, Dominic," she blurted out in a rush of shame.

His expression changed from concern to a wary watchfulness. "In what way, Carrie?" he asked softly, careful to withhold judgement.

She felt a tide of heat sweep up her neck and burn into her cheeks, and it took every ounce of her willpower to hold his gaze, despite the guilt that was making knots of her stomach. "I didn't believe you loved me," she answered bluntly.

He nodded slowly, still with that wary reservation in his eyes. "But you do now," he said.

"Yes. And I'm sorry it took so long to—"

"That doesn't matter to me, Carrie. Only having you matters," he asserted quietly.

She shook her head, her cheeks flaming even more painfully. "You don't understand, Dominic. This morning..." She took a deep breath. "This morning, when you said what you did about Alyson Hawthorn...all these years I've believed something very different."

"I realised that, Carrie," he said soothingly.

"No. You can't know. I—I made a mistake. A terrible mistake."

He rose from the sofa and gently slid his hands around her shoulders, giving them a light reassuring squeeze. His eyes were soft with compassion. "Carrie, I said I'd never criticise you and I never will," he promised her tenderly. "I know you would only have done what you believed was right at the time."

She couldn't stop the tears that blurred her eyes. She didn't deserve his understanding or his wonderful generosity, but she was intensely grateful for them.

"It was Alyson who came between us, wasn't it?" he asked gently.

"Yes." She choked the word out, working hard to swallow the growing lump in her throat. "But it wasn't only her. All the women said it was true. Every one of them. On the beach that afternoon. Although I already knew that I didn't fit in with...with your social set. Somehow I was outside them. Apart. Even so, I waited to hear it from you. For you to explain why you did what you did with me...to me. I couldn't believe it...didn't want to believe it."

"Carrie, what did they say?"

"Alyson Hawthorn was wearing an engagement ring. She said that you'd given it to her and that you were going to be married. And that I was just a little fling on the side. They said everyone—you and your friends—had that kind of casual sex...and it didn't mean anything."

"And that's why you accused me of playing musical beds."

She nodded, her eyes begging his forgiveness.

"Carrie, I swear I was never like that," he insisted earnestly. "And I never had anything to do with Alyson. She frequently gave me the come-on, but I never once took her up on it. Or showed any interest in her. Maybe that wounded her ego, or maybe she thought she'd stand a better chance with me if she could get you off the scene."

"I guess I played right into her hands," Carrie agreed sadly. "I believe you now, Dominic. But it was very convincing with the others backing her up. And when you finished surfing, you didn't come looking for me. You talked to her. Stayed with her. Sat with her and the others. And I thought then that I wasn't what you wanted. I couldn't ever be like you...like them."

"That was my fault," he murmured with a deep sigh. "I should have acted sooner." His eyes pleaded for her understanding. "I knew what was going on, the way they were treating you. That afternoon, when I came out of the water, I'd decided what to do. I wanted to take you away from them, but foolishly, in my pride, I thought that was running away. A defeat. I took Alyson by the shoulders—I wanted to throttle her—and I gave her an ultimatum. Leave you alone, or get out."

"I thought you hadn't noticed...or preferred to ignore it. That you were going back to Alyson."

The pained look that crossed his face was full of savage regret. "I noticed. But Alyson was all sweetness and light. She said you were still out shopping. Not back yet. I decided to stay with them, make my peace, so that they would be nicer to you. Underneath it all, I realised I would never have anything more to do with them after that holiday was over."

"But they were so superior."

"Oh, Carrie, it was you who was so superior. They resented and were jealous of you."

"But why?"

"Because you had what they didn't. You had a soul, Carrie. A beautiful receptive soul that knew how to love. And an innocent heart that didn't know how to put anyone down or hurt or destroy. The ring Alyson showed you was probably the engagement ring that she kept when a disillusioned friend of mine decided he didn't want to marry her. Alyson was all take and no give. She didn't care about anyone but herself. And as I lay on the sand with them that afternoon, listening to their smart remarks and sophisticated cynicism, I felt more and more ashamed to be in their company. I just wanted to be with you."

Carrie's heart ached with misery as she realised how dreadfully she had misinterpreted Dominic's actions that day. "I can only say... you looked relaxed, content to be with them."

"I did leave them, Carrie," he said, his eyes urgently seeking to impress that truth on her. "I went back to the apartment to wait for you. I waited and waited, and then began to worry that you'd somehow been involved in an accident. I rang the police but there'd been no accident reported. Then I went into the bedroom and realised there was nothing of yours lying around. . . ."

He dragged in a deep breath. "At first I couldn't believe it. You couldn't have just walked out on me without a word. I ransacked the bedroom, trying to find something, anything of yours... but there was nothing left, nothing. And I didn't have your home address. All I could remember was the suburb where you lived in Sydney. I went to the hotel where you'd stayed before you came with me, but there was no booking there in your name."

"My mother made the booking for me," Carrie remembered, her chest growing tighter and tighter at this evidence of his caring.

"There was no Miller listed." The frustration in his voice carried even more conviction. "None at all!"

"My mother's name was Wainwright. She married again after my father died."

Dominic groaned. "Carrie, there are one thousand, five hundred and twenty-seven Millers in the Sydney telephone book. Or there were, when I got around to ringing every one of them, trying to find you. But the first thing I did was fly down to Sydney, because a number of buses had already left Surfers'. I knew you'd come on a bus and I thought you'd leave on one. I met every incoming bus for weeks, even after your vacation time had ended and I knew you had to be back at work. I was sure you would step off one of them, that the next passenger had to be you. But it never was."

The pain in his voice was too real to doubt, the details of all he'd done so vivid they shamed Carrie even further. The train of circumstances that had worked against both of them meeting again was one of those cruel and merciless ironies of fate that no one could have foreseen.

"I got off the bus at Taree," Carrie explained, the ravages of her painful regret making her voice husky. "I didn't want to go straight home. I knew Mum would ask about you, because I'd rung to say I was staying on. And I wasn't ready to talk. It was all too raw, too...shaming. And then, about a week later, a group of women I'd met offered me a lift back to Sydney in their car."

"Oh, Carrie, Carrie..." He wrapped her in his arms and hugged her tightly to him. "You had nothing to be ashamed of...nothing... And I tried so hard to find you... Everything I could think of. I used to drive around the western suburbs on weekends, hoping I might spot you somewhere. I asked after you at countless restaurants. I cursed myself a thousand times for not asking more about your life instead of talking endlessly about mine."

"I wanted to hear about yours, Dominic. Mine was so narrow and ordinary. You opened a new world to me."

"An empty world...without you, Carrie."

And he kissed her like a starving man, as though time was still an enemy, and he must take what he could to fill the emptiness lest a future of plenty was only a mirage that might disappear at any moment. Carrie responded with equal passion, wanting to reassure him that she was his to have and always would be from this moment on.

"I'm sorry, Dominic," she said softly. "Sorry for all the pain I've put us both through. Because I did love you. I never stopped loving you. If only I had stayed long enough to—"

"Don't blame yourself, Carrie," he cut in with a fervour that swept away any guilt on her part. "I was so blind not to see how the situation could affect you.

What I was used to...was not for you. Nor for me, either. Although it took your leaving to open my eyes to that. Too late," he murmured regretfully.

"We have the rest of our lives," she reminded him hopefully.

His face relaxed into happy relief. "Yes, thank God! And I never thought I'd ever thank God for someone being sick, but I have, Carrie. For the sickness that brought you back to me...even though it struck horror in me at the time."

She reached up and stroked his cheek in apologetic appeal. "I'm sorry about your wife, Dominic. I didn't know about Sandra and how she died until Mrs. Coombe told me today."

He frowned.

"When she brought your guitar, I asked her," Carrie explained quickly. "I didn't know whether you were still married or not and..."

"Oh, Carrie!" Anguish twisted across his face. "Forgive me, darling. It never even occurred to me that you didn't know. Even this morning when you asked about Alyson..."

"There was a photograph of her in the newspaper, and a caption saying she was getting a divorce and marrying some other man. I thought you were free, Dominic. And that's when I called you...."

He shut his eyes tight. His jaw clenched. "My God! Do you mean to say that all my future happiness was bound up in the fluke chance of your seeing a photograph of Alyson in a newspaper?"

"Just for once, God was on our side," Carrie whispered, hoping Dominic would forgive her worst mistake as easily as he had forgiven the rest. "There's something more I've got to tell you, Dominic."

He slowly opened his eyes, looking at her with fierce resolution. "Nothing will ever separate us again, Carrie. Nothing that you or I or anyone can say will make any difference to that. I want you to marry me. Promise me now that you will. I couldn't bear to have anything more come between us. I don't care what it is you have on your mind. Say you'll marry me."

His intense forcefulness on the point swept the last of Carrie's fears away. Love and happiness billowed from her heart and radiated in her whole face. "I will. Whenever you say. I want very much to be your wife, Dominic, and share our lives together. And there's something else we share, too."

"What's that?"

"Our son."

She searched his eyes anxiously, but there was not the slightest shadow on the joy that spilled into them. And the smile that had started when she had accepted his proposal of marriage widened to a huge grin.

"So Danny *is* mine," he said with an expression of glorious satisfaction. "I felt so sure of it."

"You had it right that day we took him to your school," Carrie rushed out. "I don't know what went wrong with the precautions we took, but there was no other man, Dominic. I was afraid of what you might do if I admitted Danny was yours. I thought you were married to Alyson and—"

He threw back his head and laughed, then picked Carrie up and twirled her around as though she were a child. Although when he gathered her in his arms he quickly reminded her that she was very much a woman.

"So he *was* premature," he said exultantly. "And when you came to me asking for help to get *your* baby back from the welfare people, it was really *my* son you were asking me to help.''

''Yes, I'm sorry, Dominic.''

His eyes laughed away any concern. ''Carrie Miller, you have a hide!''

''If there had been any other way, I would have done it. I knew I was taking a high-risk step, but I was desperate, Dominic. Truly desperate.''

''You'll never be that way again, Carrie,'' he assured her. He suddenly chuckled. ''As to it being a high-risk step for you, let me tell you, I've been taking a few high-risk steps myself in my desperation to keep you in my life since that day you walked back into it. I guess luck had to fall my way sooner or later. And it did!''

She couldn't tell him she knew about the apartment and the decorating. She had given her word to Mrs. Coombe and Gina. But she loved him all the more for every step he had taken to ensure she would end up where she belonged. With him.

''You do like Danny, don't you?'' she asked anxiously.

''I love him.''

There was nothing halfhearted about that response. ''He's got your eyes,'' Carrie said ruefully.

''And my voice,'' Dominic added proudly, then laughed in sheer pleasure. ''I was dying for you to admit it last night. When you didn't, I thought it meant I had to prove a lot more to you.''

''I almost died, too. When Danny started singing. I just thought it was better to wait ... to see.''

''He likes me, Carrie.''

She laughed. ''Of course he does! How could he not? His first question this morning was about you. Whether you were coming tonight.''

"He's a great kid."

"Mmm . . . very like his father."

"When do we tell him?"

"Tonight, if you like. But it might be better to get him used to the idea of you first," she added worriedly. Danny was bound to ask some touchy questions that would take some delicate answering. Even so, she did not want to deny Dominic anything now.

"You're right. We'll approach it slowly," he agreed, immediately appreciating that some finesse was required. Then he sighed with huge satisfaction. "Tonight is the best night of my life. You...and Danny as well. When do you expect him home, Carrie?"

"Seven o'clock."

"Then we've got some time to fill, and there's still a lot I want to know about you. Why you left home and went to Fiji, what happened to your mother and the rest of your family...so much that I don't know."

They sat on the chesterfield, Carrie half-sprawled across Dominic's lap so that he could stroke her hair and kiss her when he wanted to.

She told him that she barely remembered her real father, who had died when she was six years old. They had lived in Perth then. When her mother had remarried, they had moved right across Australia to Sydney to start a new life, and she had lost all contact with her father's family. Her mother had been an English immigrant so she had no family of her own in Australia. When her second marriage ended in divorce, she was settled here and had no reason to return to Perth. She had supported Carrie through her pregnancy and minded Danny while Carrie finished her apprenticeship as a chef. Soon after that she had suffered a stroke. It had killed her.

"That must have been a dreadful shock to you ... your mother going so suddenly," Dominic murmured sympathetically.

"She left an awful hole in our lives ... mine and Danny's," Carrie acknowledged sadly. "I felt then that I couldn't stay in Sydney. It was too hard, having no one but Danny and knowing you were living so close, just across the city. The temptation to contact you was worse than ever. I thought the only way I could get on with my own life, without you haunting me all the time, was to get right away."

"So you went to Fiji," he said, a rueful irony in his eyes. "I didn't think of looking for you there, Carrie. Although I've actually been there on vacation twice in the last eight years."

"I was trying to forget you, Dominic." She sighed and stroked his cheek, her eyes reflecting his rueful irony. "But I never did. And when I came back, it wasn't only for Danny's education. Underneath it all, I wanted to be near you again."

The green eyes filled with poignant memories as she studied the face she loved so dearly. "In the song Danny sang for you, *'Isa Lei,'* there's a line—'Every moment my heart for you is yearning'—and that was how I always felt, Dominic."

"So did I," he murmured, and kissed her with all the sweetness of knowing that the long yearning had finally come to an end.

They were supremely content just to hold one another and be together, enjoying the wonderful freedom of total trust and love, knowing they could say anything or do anything and it wouldn't be misconstrued or rejected. Time flew by and they were so immersed in each other that the buzzer announcing Mrs. Coombe's arrival with Danny startled them. But their response was quick and full of joyful anticipation. Dominic stood in the lobby with Carrie, his arm around her in an extremely possessive fashion as they waited to greet their son and his minder.

The elevators doors opened.

"Dom!" Danny shrieked in surprised pleasure.

"If it's okay with you, Danny, I think we could make that Dad," Dominic declared. "Your mother has just consented to marry me." He lifted brilliant blue eyes to his secretary. "You may be the first to congratulate us, Mrs. Coombe."

"My hearty congratulations, Mr. Savage!" she enthused, stepping forward to shake Dominic's hand. Then she clasped Carrie's, her grey eyes glinting maxi approval.

"Does this mean you're going to be my father for always?" Danny asked, almost jumping out of his skin with excitement.

"Absolutely," Dominic confirmed. "You're stuck with me for life, Danny."

"That's great! I always wanted a dad. You've done real good, Mum."

Carrie had to laugh. "Thank you, Danny." Dominic had handled the matter beautifully, just as he handled everything beautifully. Later on, after their relationship was cemented, would be time enough to reveal that Dominic was Danny's real father. Let the trust between them build....

"Very good, indeed!" Mrs. Coombe agreed, beaming approval at all of them. "I must be going now. A happy night to all of you."

"Thank you, Mrs. Coombe," they chorussed in joyful unison.

She stepped into the elevator, and to Carrie's eyes she seemed to emanate an aura of bright benevolence. Not a dragon, Carrie thought. Nor a sergeant-major. Nor even a good watchdog. A fairy godmother, that's what she was, underneath all the iron-plated armour.

Then the doors closed on her.

But she left behind the magic.

"Well," said Dominic. "I brought my guitar, Danny. How about a song?"

"Yes, sir!" Danny yelled and dived past them into the living room as he spied the guitar case.

Dominic's arm tightened around Carrie's shoulders as they followed their son. "Shall we try the Allelujah Chorus?" he mused softly to her.

"Can you play it on guitar?"

"No. But it's singing in my heart."

"In mine, too."

"How would you like a honeymoon in Fiji?"

"Nanuya Bay?"

"Absolutely."

"That would be the loveliest place in the world."

"That's where your friends are. We'll go there often, Carrie."

They smiled at each other, knowing that nothing on earth would ever separate them again. Their togetherness was complete.

HARLEQUIN

Romance®

announces

THE BRIDAL COLLECTION

one special Romance
every month,
featuring
a Bride, a Groom and a Wedding!

Beginning in May 1992
with
The Man You'll Marry
by Debbie Macomber

WED-1

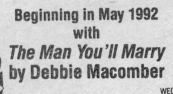

Following the success of **WITH THIS RING**, Harlequin cordially invites you to enjoy the romance of the wedding season with

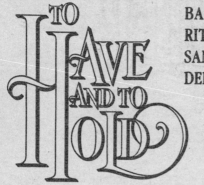

BARBARA BRETTON
RITA CLAY ESTRADA
SANDRA JAMES
DEBBIE MACOMBER

A collection of romantic stories that celebrate the joy, excitement, and mishaps of planning that special day by these four award-winning Harlequin authors.

Available in April at your favorite Harlequin retail outlets.

THTH

HARLEQUIN PROUDLY PRESENTS A
DAZZLING CONCEPT IN ROMANCE FICTION

One small town,
twelve terrific love stories.

TYLER—GREAT READING…GREAT SAVINGS…
AND A FABULOUS FREE GIFT

Each book set in Tyler is a self-contained love story;
together, the twelve novels stitch the fabric of
the community.

By collecting proofs-of-purchase found in each Tyler
book, you can receive a fabulous gift, ABSOLUTELY
FREE! And use our special Tyler coupons to save on
your next Tyler book purchase.

Join us for the third Tyler book, WISCONSIN
WEDDING by Carla Neggers, available in May.
